Magnolia Mistletoe

An Edisto Christmas Novella

by

LINDSEY P. BRACKETT

FIREFLY
SOUTHERN FICTION
LIGHTHOUSE PUBLISHING OF THE CAROLINAS

MAGNOLIA MISTLETOE BY LINDSEY BRACKETT
Firefly Southern Fiction is an imprint of LPCBooks
a division of Iron Stream Media
100 Missionary Ridge, Birmingham, AL 35242

ISBN: 978-1-64526-291-6
Copyright © 2020 by J. Lindsey Brackett
Cover design by Lindsey Brackett and Hannah Linder
Interior design by Karthick Srinivasan

Available in print from your local bookstore, online, or from the
publisher at: LPCbooks.com

For more information on this book and the author visit:
LindseyPBrackett.com

Library of Congress Cataloging-in-Publication Data
Brackett, Lindsey.
Magnolia Mistletoe / Lindsey Brackett 1st ed.

Printed in the United States of America

DEDICATION

For Heather
who knows how to plan a party,
especially an Edisto one.

Many, many thanks and Christmas cookies go to the
following editors and readers who helped make this book
possible:

Leslie DeVooght
Kimberly Duffy
Leslie McKee
Jennifer Slattery

Chapter One

December 2006

Fidgeting, especially while holding an umbrella the size of South Carolina, was not an option.

Hannah gritted her teeth. A trickle of rainwater slid under the collar of her black Banana Republic dress. No matter, the bridesmaids' silk gowns must remain immaculate.

Carolina Calhoun Events had planned hundreds of Charlestonian weddings, but this one—dripping through the last of an Atlantic tropical storm—would no doubt be retold over cocktails for years to come.

Her mother—Carolina herself—cut her eyes at Hannah when she gave in and twitched a shoulder. She stilled. This fiasco could be called her fault, too. She'd sided with the bride about not moving the ceremony indoors, believing they could surely get seventy-five guests under the wide portico of the family's West Ashley mansion.

December's descent upon the South Carolina coast may have required umbrellas over scarves, but according to Charleston's local forecast, the rain would move out in the next twenty minutes. In time for dinner and dancing, and hopefully before Hannah dissolved into a soggy mess.

Or a puddle of regret. Which was all she'd been to her mother for the past six months.

As the ceremony ended and the bridal party headed back inside until the official introductions, Hannah melted into the edge of the crowd. She held the umbrella like a shield in case the wind shifted and drenched the guests who mingled among the white folding chairs.

Her mother's voice demurred in her ear, the headset's channel clear. "Very nice. Emmie, send out the servers and let's help these people forget the weather."

Emmie. Her mother's new pet project. Carolina Calhoun could take even the most awkward of interns and turn them into sophisticated designers. After all, her magic had started with Hannah.

Though rebellion maybe wasn't the same as social anxiety.

Servers in vests and bowties wove through the crowd, passing out bourbon and bacon-wrapped scallops. Sunlight broke through the clouds as the last of the rain slacked away. Flooded with relief, Hannah lowered her umbrella and began ushering guests down the pebbled garden path to the large tent already set with linens and china for dinner.

"I still believe we should've moved the ceremony out here." Her mother slipped beside her. Too professional to chastise Hannah over the headset, she kept her voice low and even. "Wouldn't have been any more crowded. Lost the view as it is, under the porch like that." She waved a hand at the Intercoastal Waterway, sparkling now under the setting sun.

"You always say give the bride what she wants."

"Here's why I know you're not ready to go out on your own, Hannah, much as that may help our ... situation."

Situation. Hannah swallowed the lump in her throat.

Mistake. She'd made a mistake over two dozen weddings ago.

Her mother tapped one manicured finger on her clipboard of notes. "Brides must be told what they want, especially when their desires put your plans one step from disaster." Her mother's blue eyes—the color of all the women in their family—regarded her warily. "And Hannah, honey, it's your job to avoid disaster."

Except disaster and Hannah went hand in hand.

Her cousin, logical and organized Cora Anne, said this was because Hannah led with her heart instead of her head. Which ought to be a positive characteristic for someone who planned happily ever after for a living.

Even if she had no prospect of her own hovering on the horizon. She'd thought—after their summer on Edisto—Ben might have called. His best friend was likely to marry her cousin, soon as Cora Anne saw the light, came home from Tulane University, and parked herself back in the Lowcountry where she belonged.

At least that's what Hannah hoped. Selfishly, maybe, because texting was not the same as girl talk over lattes.

Mom glanced at her watch. "Time to introduce the bridal party."

Relieved for a chance to escape more disapproval, Hannah nodded. "I'll tell the DJ." Once, her mother had forgiven her escapades more easily. After all, Carolina Calhoun hadn't been all that levelheaded herself in her youth. But Hannah couldn't blame her, really. She'd risked hers, her mother's, and the business's reputation with that frolic at the Gibbes's wedding.

She strode toward the gazebo housing the band. Cutting across the lawn, she wouldn't have to sidestep guests along the path that, conveniently for them, would keep their shoes dry. But just as she reached her destination, the heel of her favorite black pumps sank into the soft mud and seemed determined to stay there.

Disaster. Of course.

"Need a hand?" A familiar voice, laughter underscoring its tone, came out of the garden shadows. Benjamin Townsend, roguishly handsome as ever in a sport coat and tie, emerged from an arbor.

Surely the day's stress had caused her to hallucinate. She'd memorized the guest list, and he wasn't on it.

He slipped a hand under her elbow. "How are you, Hannah?"

Cheeks flushing, surely from embarrassment, she smoothed her dress and forced a smile, still subtly wiggling her trapped heel. "I'm wonderful, Ben. How are you?"

He cocked an eyebrow. "Are you so wonderful you want me to leave you stuck right here?"

She sighed. "If you'll just—"

He lifted her by the waist and twirled her back onto the path. Balancing on one foot—and fighting her quivering stomach—Hannah waited for him to retrieve her shoe. When he did, he bent and slipped it onto her foot. "Now you can be wonderful again."

"Thank you." She ducked her head to adjust the heel—and hide her flushed cheeks.

"So this is one of your shindigs, huh?" He waved to indicate the festivities. Twinkling lights, magnolia garlands, and poinsettia centerpieces set the Christmas wedding ambiance.

She straightened her spine. "Shindig, no. A Carolina Calhoun wedding is a well-oiled machine."

"Point taken."

Between him and the rain and her mother's tight smiles, Hannah wanted to explode. But she forced a smile, as if glad to see him. Which she didn't want to be. "What are you doing here?"

"I brought Christy because Jared's out of town." Ben nodded toward his beautiful blond sister. Christy, spotting Hannah, disentangled herself from another guest—a prominent Charleston daughter Hannah recognized from the one event she wanted to forget.

"Hannah, so good to see you." Christy clasped Hannah's hands. "When are you getting back out to Edisto? We've missed you at the beach."

Hannah dared a glance toward Ben. Missed her indeed. Not enough to call, apparently. "Soon, I'm sure. Mom and Aunt Lou have been planning the family's Christmas Eve party for weeks."

Christy engulfed her in a hug. "I know this will be a hard one, with your Nan gone." Her embrace had the warmth of a sister, settling Hannah's agitation.

"Thank you."

"I must get back to my friends. I haven't seen some of these girls in years. Can you believe I've known Kathleen Rutledge since we were eight years old? And now we're both married." Christy shook her blond curls in disbelief. "You must just love your job, Hannah. Experiencing wedding joy all the time."

"The joy is good." She rubbed her still-damp neck. "But some are drier than others."

Laughing, Christy squeezed her hand and retreated back to her friends. Hannah pirouetted and surveyed the scene. Everything appeared under control, even as her mother's voice spoke in her ear. "Hannah, have you cued the band for the entrance yet?"

5

Ben turned with her toward the gazebo. "I'm betting the Rutledges weren't one of your easiest clients."

"Whatever gives you that idea?"

"There's a little worry line right here." Drawing her back, he tapped her forehead between her eyes. Hannah pulled away, throat dry. That touch carried familiarity, but friends didn't go three months without speaking.

"I'm fine. Everything's fine."

"Hmmm…" He shook his head, and a lock of brown hair bounced on his brow. "Fine is one of those words negated when said twice."

"Then I'll say it again just to prove my point. Everything"—she looked him square in his mischievous hazel eyes—"is going *fine*. If you'll excuse me, please."

As she descended the gazebo's steps after the cue, Emmie intercepted her. "Hannah." The girl's eyes were wide, darting frantically.

"What now?"

"The bartender," Emmie leaned in to whisper through clenched teeth, "is sick."

Was the girl always this dramatic? "Sick how?"

"He got sick"—Emmie waved her hand—"in the bushes."

Fine. Hannah squeezed a fist as she thought the word. For this there could be a little panic. "Send him home. Does the caterer have a backup?"

Emmie's head jerked side to side. "No. He said he was already short-staffed tonight."

"Great." Hannah cast her eyes to the sky now dotting with stars. Then she glanced around, as if an answer might appear in the bushes. Her gaze collided with Ben's. He still hovered under the arbor. Carolina's favorite florist had enhanced it with mistletoe and curling red ribbon, setting the scene for a Christmas romance.

How long had he been watching her?

"Get rid of the sick guy, Emmie, before he's worse." She took her intern by the shoulders and turned her around. "I've got a plan."

Benjamin Townsend was about to have something else to occupy his thoughts. She'd show him fine.

***

Of course he didn't mind tending bar.

Something to do with his hands and plenty of opportunity for his eyes to track across this manicured spectacle and land on Hannah Calhoun. She never flustered, never stuttered, no matter the situation. If he hadn't witnessed her stumble himself, he'd never believe she ever wobbled on those high heels that made her legs impossibly long.

Ben poured a Jack and Coke for one of the groomsmen who'd already lost his bowtie. "Have a good one."

Instead of moving on, the guy gulped big and leaned on the counter. "Think it'll be a while before I have one of those."

He couldn't have been more than twenty-five. Too young for the haunted look Ben knew by heart. "No date tonight?" He could play the bartender role. He'd perfected it in the last year owning his own restaurant.

The guy swallowed again and the drink was gone. "A date is hardly the problem." He waved at a group of women—a mix of bridesmaids and guests gathering for the ubiquitous Conga line, no doubt. Setting his empty glass down, he added, "Must be nice to have a job that doesn't depend on market trends and stocks."

Ben refreshed the drink. "Heard things might be

taking a dip." Five years later, and the economy's 9/11 effects lingered on.

"A dip?" The guy's laugh was brittle. "More like a nosedive right out of the sky. I'll give you a tip that's better than this jar." He leaned in, pushing aside the glass vase full of cash. "If you've got money sunk into real estate, better get out while the gettin's good because this whole world is built on a house of cards." With that, he flicked a five into the tip jar and strode away.

"You shouldn't frown so at the guests."

Ben met Hannah's look square on. In the twinkle lights' glow, her perfect blue eyes sparkled. Softer now that the evening was winding down with no more mishaps. "Not all of them are worth a smile." He gave her one just to prove his point, but she broke their eye contact.

So much for flirting with the help.

"Thanks for doing this. We really appreciate it."

"Happy to be of assistance." He'd be even happier to be her ride home, but he'd realized after their summer, Hannah Calhoun was dangerous. Too much happily ever after in her world.

Too little in his.

Chapter Two

"In the end, all turned out lovely." Mom flipped through the ancient Rolodex she still insisted upon using. "And wasn't it kind of Ben to help?"

Hannah tapped a pencil against her palm. They had to change venues for the Barron wedding. Who knew such a tiny kitchen fire could shut down a whole country club? Three weeks until Christmas meant everything was already booked. Right now they had bigger fish to fry than Ben Townsend's cordiality.

The thought hit her like one of those waves crashing off the Edisto shore.

"Here, how about the Yacht Club?" Her mother pulled a card from the file and helped herself to one of the gingerbread scones Hannah had brought in from the bakery on King Street.

"They're booked. Emmie already called." Hannah twisted in the swivel chair and stood, knees a little shaky. The stress of a venue change meant she'd indulged in two of those seasonal treats. Clearly the sugar was affecting her, not the place she was about to suggest. "How about The Hideaway?"

"Ben's place on Edisto?" Her mother's fair brows rose. "You'd have to talk to him."

Talking wasn't the problem. Thinking about him on the other hand ... Hannah crossed her arms. "He's told me before he'd be interested in hosting some events. It's not exactly beach season, so I'm betting they're available."

Mom plucked back her Yacht Club card. "This is Christmas. Season of miracles. Let's see you work one, Miss I Can Do This by Myself."

Hannah bit her lip. It had been months since her mother seriously considered her idea. "I would like to go out on my own. Someday."

"You handled the weekend well. Better than I expected, honestly." Her mother cupped Hannah's cheek. "There's no doubt you have a gift for this. But you need to show me you're ready, that you won't be swayed by emotions again. Working with Ben might be a good place to start."

She opened her mouth to protest, but Mom held up a finger. "Don't even try to tell me there's not a spark there, hon. Romance is how I make my living, remember? All I'm saying is, it's Christmas, so don't get caught under the mistletoe with a vendor."

"Mom…" She chewed her lip, still sweet with the scone's cream cheese drizzle, and tried not to think about Ben's daring grin. "I'll be careful."

But she waited until her mother went into the back room to count linens before pulling a business card from her blazer pocket. Fingering its edge, she remembered the light in Ben's eyes when he'd passed it over and told her to call anytime.

About business, of course. Which picnics on the beach and sunset river rides in a johnboat most definitely were not.

***

"So I told her yes, of course." Ben stretched his legs and propped his feet on the deck railing but kept the bag of boiled peanuts within reach. Besides Santa in short sleeves, the best thing about mild Lowcountry winters was the roadside stands rarely closed up shop.

"Of course." Beside him, Tennessee Watson stretched as well but kept his booted feet on the ground. A fine layer of sawdust covered his clothes. Ben would've already showered and changed, but Tennessee wore construction debris like a second skin.

"Could be a good little side venture, tide us over till this storm passes." Ben tapped one shiny new shoe against the other and sucked salt off the soft peanut shells.

Beyond his back deck, the sun settled down, streaking the sky burnt orange and deep pink. Hannah had a dress that color. She'd been wearing it the first night he met her, sharing shrimp dip and stories with her cousin at The Hideaway.

But the black number she'd had on Saturday night had made him seriously consider catching her under that arbor of magnolia and mistletoe.

"Could be that." Tennessee's agreement brought Ben back to reality. "But if the rumors are true, what we really need to do is unload some of the real estate. I don't want to be sitting on a half-dozen unsold homes." He scrubbed a hand through his blond hair and frowned. His eyes had taken on a calculating look Ben knew all too well.

"You want to drop the prices? We're already more than fair on market value." Nothing he hated more than losing. Money. Investments. Women.

"If we drop 'em, does it make us look like we're panicking?" Tennessee leaned forward, elbows on his knees.

"Nah." Ben dropped his feet back to the porch. Panic he'd given up long ago. "Just makes us look like we're moving on to the next big thing." A look he'd cultivated in the past few years.

"I don't think there's going to be a next big thing anytime soon."

He punched his best friend's shoulder. "Lighten up. You want to worry about a home, worry about which one you're going to offer Cora Anne alongside that ring I know you've got picked out and waiting."

Tennessee slid him a glance. "I haven't picked out a ring—yet. And don't you dare breathe a word to Hannah when you meet with her tomorrow. Those two are thicker than thieves."

"I promise to only talk one wedding with Hannah. The one she's paying us to host."

"You might want to talk something else with her." Tennessee rolled his shoulders, leaning back.

"Referral fee?"

"Or why you never called?"

Ben sputtered, a peanut lodged in his throat.

Tennessee smacked him between the shoulder blades. "Man, you better watch out. Ain't nothing like being in deep water with a Coultrie girl."

Ben linked his fingers behind his head and breathed in deep the smell of pluff mud and independence. Despite the loss of the girls' grandmother, the Coultrie family's presence lingered on Edisto Island. In the old farm up Highway 174, Cora Anne's mother had retreated, and on the point at the beach, Still Waters stood, a family cottage that exhibited some of Tennessee's finest work.

Tennessee, he fit in nicely with the Coultries, even if their pasts were all tangled together like a shrimp net that hadn't been spread out proper. They'd all had fun over the summer, but Ben didn't need the pressure of another close-knit family. His own had proven quite enough.

Right on cue, his friend added, "Heard from Bill yet?"

Ben tossed a handful of shells off the deck and stood. "He'll call by Christmas. Always does." He didn't add that his father would ask for money, and Ben would send it for only one reason.

To keep him from ever coming back.

Chapter Three

"Ceremony here, facing the water." On The Hideaway's dock, Hannah faced away from Big Bay Creek and waved her arms in what Ben assumed was an indication of seating. When she stepped backward, he restrained himself from lunging forward in case she tripped off the edge. Those heels were going to get the girl in big trouble someday.

But Hannah stepped flawlessly.

Ben shoved his hands in his pockets. Her stumble at the wedding was clearly out of the norm. Besides, he didn't need another excuse to touch her when he, after all, hadn't bothered to call.

"Ben, what do you think?"

He blinked. What did he think about what?

"An arbor on the dock. All right with you?" Hannah propped her hands on her narrow hips. She'd kept a smile for the clients, but she looked at him like he'd just eaten the last of the homemade peach ice cream.

"Arbor's fine. Whatever y'all want." He turned from Hannah and spoke to the bride and her mother. Both wore pearls and smelled like Neiman Marcus, a place he would rather avoid. But expensive perfume translated to deep pockets. "We're just here to make this day unforgettable."

"I can't believe how lovely this is," the bride gushed. "That fire's turning into a real blessing."

Blessing indeed. He had quickly researched comparable venues before naming his price to Hannah earlier. She hadn't so much as flinched, pronouncing it fair and suggesting that once a few events had been executed successfully, he might even raise it. The real estate bubble might be threatening to burst, but evidently the wedding business remained solid.

Well, people did love a party.

"Ben, can we go inside now?" Hannah appeared at his elbow, brows raised and sparks in her blue eyes. *Pay attention*, those eyes snapped.

"Of course." He led the little group around front, and they climbed the wide steps. Ben pointed out the handicapped-accessible ramp on the side, and Hannah explained she thought they'd do a hot chocolate bar right out here on the wide porch. "Will save room inside and if it's chilly, people will love having something warm while they mingle."

"Oh, and the favors, too, right?" Jana, the bride— Ben finally remembered her name—squeezed her mother's arm. "I'm loving all this."

"Yes, favors, too." Hannah waited for Ben to open and hold the heavy oak door before stepping aside and letting Jana and her mother enter.

"Mom, this is perfect." Jana walked a slow rotation around the dining room. Her mother followed, chin high as though on an inspection.

Ben knew pride made him stand a little taller, even though the craftsmanship had been all Tennessee. Original heart pine floors complemented walls stained the color of warm honey and accented by lantern sconces, his mother's contribution. After Thanksgiving, Christy and his mother had looped magnolia garland

16

around the doorways and wide bar. There were wreaths on the windows giving the whole place an ambiance of rustic chic—so his mother said.

But Ben knew The Hideaway's true ambiance. After all, he'd chosen the thing that made it so special. Location. An unending vista of Big Bay Creek opened into the Intercoastal Waterway, spartina grass swaying in the breeze. Once people came and saw, they came again.

"Are you sure there will be enough room?" The bride's mother finally spoke, as though she felt the need to temper her daughter's exuberance.

"Positive, ma'am. Out here"—Ben pushed open the French doors that separated the dining room from the screened porch—"I thought we'd break down all these tables and set you up for dancing. I've got heaters if we need them, because you never know when the weather's going to turn into actual winter."

"Thank you." Ben nearly stumbled as the young woman flung her arms around him. "My wedding is going to be amazing."

Hannah met his gaze with a grin of satisfaction.

***

Hannah spent two hours meticulously planning every new detail. She walked the property at least a half-dozen times, taking notes and drawing diagrams. The sun had begun its slow descent over the marsh by the time she stuck her head in the kitchen door to tell Ben she was leaving.

On the stainless-steel counter, a scattering of ledgers and receipts surrounded his open laptop. The rich smell of butter and garlic made her inhale deeply.

"I'm multitasking." He uncorked a bottle of wine.

"Want to stay and help?"

She bit her lip, but this was just business. After all, over half her list was for him. Sliding onto a stool, she crossed her ankles for propriety and composure and accepted the glass he offered. "You sure won them over."

"Charming the ladies is a specialty of mine." He grated Parmesan over a bowl of pasta, one impish brown lock bouncing on his forehead as he concentrated. Hannah glanced away.

His charms were all too familiar.

The pasta was laden with cream sauce and tiny creek shrimp. "You picking up the slack in the kitchen these days?"

Ben shrugged. "Just a hobby. Talked Gavin, my chef, into showing me a few things."

"Speaking of Gavin, he's good with this menu?" She flipped a page on her clipboard.

"Called him while you were outside making my honey-do list." Her cheeks heated, but he had turned back to the stove to dish up his own supper. "He says it's pretty basic, but we'll need plenty of servers. Told me to hire a couple extras because he wants some of ours in the kitchen with him." He sat across from her and opened a beer. "Hand me some silverware?"

She passed over the rolled linen napkin, careful to avoid a touch. "Have anyone in mind, or you want me to make some calls? We have a list." She twirled her fork through the pasta and took a bite, the crescendo of simple flavors reminding her of Nan in the most tangible way. "Wow."

Ben's grin widened. "I keep telling Gavin to let me make this one night. I'm ready."

"I agree." She reached for her wine though she already

felt the buzz of good food and good company. "All I can cook is scrambled eggs and toast."

Ben shook his head. "Having known your grandmother, I seriously doubt that. "

"It's true. Nan only domesticated Cora Anne this summer. She must have figured someday my cousin will need to know how to make crab cakes and fry chicken out here away from everything."

"Away from everything?" Ben snapped his napkin at her, and she dodged the blow, laughing. "We've got everything we need right here on Edisto. Can just live off the land."

"Mm-hmm. That's why my mama always packed two coolers full of essentials"—she made quotes in the air with her fingers—"whenever we came for the summer."

Ben grabbed the wine and topped off her glass. "Uh-huh. Some people just don't appreciate the fine assortment the Piggly Wiggly has to offer."

She propped her elbows on the counter, leaning toward camaraderie over formality. "Mom likes to remind me there was a time when Whaley's was the only place on the island you could buy ice and beer, and that when she was a child, almost all their food came from the farm. Self-sustainability."

Ben nodded. "Farm-to-table before it was trending."

"Seems to have caught on well here, for you."

He shrugged and ate for a moment. "We're doing pretty good. Hope it continues." But the way he picked up his beer and shifted it hand to hand indicated otherwise. "Can I ask you something?"

Twirling her fork through the remaining noodles, Hannah nodded. His tone had deepened, and with it, trepidation came creeping up her spine like the mists stealing over the marsh as night settled in.

"You think she's coming back?"

"Cora Anne?" Realization doused cold like the ocean's winter waves. He must be looking out for Tennessee. Just a business dinner indeed.

"Yeah." Ben hung the bottle loosely between his fingers. "Or is he kidding himself?"

Hannah tossed her bangs from her eyes. Time for a trim and time to move on. "Aunt Lou says she'll be home for Christmas."

"So anytime now?"

"I guess." She pushed her plate aside. "But there's a wedding in two weeks, so if you want to worry about something, worry about that."

"I'm not worried."

Of course not. "You want to go over this list now or have me email you?"

His hazel eyes probed hers for the first time all evening, as though he finally sensed he'd blundered. "Email's awfully cold, Hannah. Especially since I made you dinner and all."

She sat back, arms crossed. How did he always set her off kilter? "Thank you for that."

"Why do I get the feeling you're mad at me?"

"I'm not."

"Not what I heard." Ben raised his brows and his bottle.

Heat swept her cheeks. Couldn't tell Cora Anne anything anymore.

"Well, I thought you might call. That we might..." Stop. She would not beg. "Be friends." Her fingers tightened on the stem of her glass.

"Just friends?"

She widened her eyes. Time he was the one off balance. "Did you think more?"

He stood, clearing plates. "No, but I got the impression…" He turned, set the plates in the sink, but his hand lingered, as if drawing resolve from the stainless steel. "I'm not really looking for a relationship, Hannah. Not like what Tennessee and Cora Anne have going." Facing her again, he retrieved his beer. "I mean, I think they're great, and I'm real happy for them, if it works out. But I'm just having a good time right now."

Hannah nodded, her throat thick with cream sauce and good wine. Not hurt. "Right. Me, too."

"Yeah?" He tipped his chin, kept his eyes steady on hers.

She refused to look away. "Sure. I'm only interested in planning other people's weddings. So let's get to it, all right?"

Chapter Four

"You're a fool, man." Tennessee clipped a fuzzy reindeer antler into place on the cab of his truck. Across the roof, Ben attached the other.

"I'm not headed for some happily ever after just because you are," Ben said, stepping back to admire their work. Big red nose on the grille and they'd be ready for the annual Edisto Beach Christmas Parade. "I like Hannah—she's good company and all—but I'm not settling down anytime soon."

"You're an idiot."

"Maybe," he conceded. But storybook endings belonged to those who believed in happily ever after.

The December morning had risen with a bit of chill, but now the sun beamed thin rays of warmth through his windbreaker. Perfect day for fishing. However, the parade started in an hour, and they'd been charged not only with participating but pulling the float for the Presbyterian Church preschool.

Excellent community service, Ben figured. He'd even let Christy and the kids make a round of green and red paper chains to ring the truck's bed. Though he'd drawn the line when his sister requested he wear his stepfather's Santa suit.

Entrants had lined up at block 600 on Palmetto Boulevard, and already the crowd was spilling over the cracked sidewalks. Ben waved at his mother and stepfather as they unfolded camp chairs for a prime seat. With them was Tennessee's mother, Grace, and a host of other church folks, all sporting antler headbands that matched the ones they'd clipped over the truck's doors. He leaned against the tailgate studying the fire trucks, golf carts, and even boats representing all manner of Edisto businesses and livelihoods this year.

"If you're posing for a picture, I think it's already been taken."

Ben snapped his neck around and found Hannah eyeing him with a smirk. She jerked that saucy chin at the magnetic sign on the truck's side, which advertised Benjamin Townsend, Realtor, with a large full-color image of him propped against the tailgate, arms crossed.

He dropped the pose, shoving his hands in his pockets, mostly because he had the urge to reach for hers. "You come to watch the parade?"

She set a finger to her lips and pointed behind him. "And the reunion."

Glancing over his shoulder, he saw Tennessee adjusting the sign advertising Watson Custom Homes on the driver's door, his back to the crowd. Cora Anne snuck behind him and tapped his shoulder. Tennessee spun and, with a yelp, swooped her into an embrace.

"Maybe they should get a room." Ben turned back to Hannah.

She swatted his arm. "I think they're getting rings first."

"Right about that."

She grabbed his elbow. "You better give me the heads-up when the proposal's coming. You've seen what goes into wedding planning."

Her playful touch had him wondering what it would be like to hold her—the way his best friend currently held her cousin. Against his better judgment, he put his lips to her ear. "You sure you can keep a secret?"

She turned her head, and if he hadn't pulled back, his lips would've grazed her cheek. Her blue eyes darkened as they settled on his. "I'm quite good at keeping secrets, thank you." She walked a few steps and reached up to tweak the antler. "Is this a new marketing technique?"

"Good for business."

"Do you ever think about anything other than business?" Her eyes moved off his.

Did he? Sure. Did he like to? "Nope. This brilliant mind never rests."

She rolled her eyes, and the tension between them dissipated. "Good thing because I need to do another walk-through this afternoon. Nail down some more specifics."

So much for catching his supper. "Do *you* ever think about anything besides business?"

"If I did, I might never have my own someday."

Before he could ask about that plan, Tennessee called his name. "Hey, we about ready?" His partner had his girl tucked tight into his side, and far as Ben could tell, no intention of letting go. Yet another reason he didn't need to stir anything up with Hannah. Ben was an expert at letting go.

Hannah pushed off the truck. "Hey, Cor. You about ready to get a seat with a view?"

"How about up close to the action?" Tennessee wound both arms around Cora Anne's waist. "Want to ride in the truck?"

"With my favorite community-minded contractor?

You know it." Cora Anne flashed a smile so sunny-wide, Ben knew he and Hannah were forgotten. She looked at him, brows raised.

"We'll take the back and skip the PDA. Protect the children's eyes, you know." Ben socked his friend in the arm and pretended to check the trailer hitch. So much for getting away from Hannah Calhoun and how she always smelled of gardenias.

***

In the bed of Tennessee's truck, Hannah found her back pressed against the cab and her hip pressed against Ben's. She'd definitely had worse views of the parade.

Because the preschool teachers decided there were too many kids for everyone to sit safely on the float, the smaller children clambered up with their parents, who no doubt presumed the truck bed provided less chance of escape and kept them farther from the candy tossing.

They presumed wrong since Ben had filched a Piggly Wiggly bag full of suckers and promptly started sharing.

"Save some for the parade." Christy admonished her brother as she climbed up with her son and daughter. "Hey, there Hannah. See you got roped into all the Christmas fun."

"Nonsense is more like it." Ben's lips were at her ear again.

"I do love a good parade." Hannah shifted as Christy tilted her head, eyes sliding back and forth between her and Ben. Colby climbed up his uncle's back like a monkey, but Elizabeth pulled away from her mother and came to Hannah.

"Hi." She fluttered her long lashes. "You have pretty earrings."

Hannah fingered the beaded dangle. "Thank you. They're my favorite."

"Are you friends with Uncle Benny?"

"Um…" She glanced at Ben, who raised his brows in a *well, go on* gesture. "Sure, we are. I'm Cora Anne's cousin."

"I like Cora Anne. She has pretty earrings, too."

"You know what? I bought those for her."

Elizabeth giggled. "Mommy, can I sit with Hannah?"

"Sure, baby. If Hannah doesn't mind."

Elizabeth settled in her lap. She tried not to swoon over the little girl's green bow and darling smocked dress.

"Since y'all got this"—Christy beamed at her brother—"I'm just going to sit on the curb with my honey."

A tall, lanky man in a pressed polo and khakis lifted her down. "Thanks, bro. We never get alone time." He reached over the wheel well to greet Hannah. "Jared Aiken."

"Nice to meet you." Hannah leaned across Ben to greet his brother-in-law, but when she moved back, her bracelet snagged on his jacket.

"Hold on, I'll get it." He shrugged out of the coat. She reached to work the clasp free, but he circled her wrist with his fingers. "I said, I got it." His deft touch loosened the bracelet quickly, but he held her wrist a moment longer. "Second time I've rescued you from wardrobe malfunctions."

Her heartbeat drummed. *Just business* ran like a ticker tape in her mind. Pulling back, she tossed her head away from his, satisfied when her dangly earring grazed his cheek, lightening the moment. "So sorry for your inconvenience."

He tickled Colby under his arms, and the little boy squealed. "Who said anything about inconvenience?"

His perfect smile—and the sudden lurch of the truck forward as the parade began—threw her off balance. He pressed his shoulder against hers and left it there, keeping her stable.

Physically at least.

They rolled down Palmetto Boulevard, salt breeze lifting curls and tickling noses. Ben finally got Colby under control with the aid of a red sucker and a strong grip. He jerked his head at the ensuing chaos of the truck. "Ready to sign up for next year?"

"Do you really think it's all nonsense?" The question popped out—unlike Santa and certain members of her family, Hannah wasn't prone to checking things twice.

Ben shrugged against her shoulder. "Do you believe in every wedding you plan?"

"That's not the same thing."

"Plenty of similarities. People want to convey a certain image at Christmas—and weddings—of the perfect family." He turned his head toward hers. "Of true love."

"And you don't believe in those things?"

For a moment, the light in his usual mischievous eyes dimmed. But the sadness flitted over his features so quickly, Hannah almost thought she imagined it. "I just believe they're harder to come by then people realize."

She wanted to say true love might be worth the effort, but what did she know?

The heavy moment dissipated as Colby offered his uncle the remainder of his sucker. Hannah laughed as Ben's lip curled. "Thanks, bud. Believe I'll just keep this over here." He tossed the stick back in the Piggly Wiggly bag now full of empty candy wrappers. "So, walk-through? How long do we need?"

"At least an hour. Maybe two."

Ben tipped his face to the clear blue sky. "Guess I'll fish tomorrow, then." He grinned back at her. "You sticking around for the weekend?"

She bit her lip, wondering why he cared. She really shouldn't, but Cora Anne had convinced her to throw an overnight bag in the car. Said they could stay at Still Waters and drink tea on the deck before church. "Looks that way."

"Then let's do business today and play tomorrow. I promised you a ride on the boat, remember?"

As his hazel eyes settled on hers, all warmth and mischief, she wished she'd forgotten.

Because it might be she was a fool to remember.

Chapter Five

Hannah had worked her candy cane into a sharp point of peppermint. And she only had one sentence of a mission statement. Writing a business plan proved harder than she'd imagined.

Hannah Calhoun Weddings & Events will serve the modern bride's taste for rustic elegance paired with classic sophistication.

Well at least she could use adjectives appropriately.

She bit off the candy cane's end and crunched. Ben had filled her hands with the leftovers as she left The Hideaway that afternoon. Stupid that such a simple gesture made her giddy.

Even more ridiculous, she had spent the first hour alone at the beach cottage planning her outfit for tomorrow. No easy task since the overnight bag she'd thrown together last minute hadn't accounted for a winter boat ride.

Setting the candy aside, she picked up her pencil. She could do this. No big deal. Hadn't she been planning weddings with her mother since she was sixteen? The pencil scratched across the page.

Events of all sizes will receive personal attention and detailed analysis for quality and execution.

That made her sound like an accountant, not an event planner.

The cottage's back door rattled, and Cora Anne came in, flushed. "Hey, there. Why are you still up?" Her cousin dumped her purse and jacket on the table in a heap and crossed to the cottage's tiny kitchen. "Want some tea?"

Hannah folded her arms across her chest, back toward the kitchen. "I would but I already had two cups waiting for you. Remember we had sleepover plans?"

Cora Anne dropped into an empty seat beside her, eyes soft. "I'm sorry."

She bit off another piece of peppermint before sighing. Cora Anne's sad face rivaled the flower girl's she'd chastised last wedding. "It's okay. I just miss you, too."

"Well, good thing I'm coming back."

She grabbed her cousin's arms. "For real and permanent?"

"Transferring to the College of Charleston. I was going to tell you after—"

Leaping up and dragging Cora Anne with her, Hannah danced into the kitchen. "You're forgiven. This calls for champagne."

"Good luck finding that here."

She threw open the pantry, appraised the shelves, and decided. "We'll have to settle for possibly stale Oreos."

"Or candy canes, apparently." Cora Anne lifted the bowl Hannah had filled earlier. "I thought Ben kept all the leftovers."

"No, he gave them to me."

The kettle whistled, sparing Hannah her cousin's scrutiny. Cora Anne poured her tea while Hannah settled back at the table, twisting Oreos apart. Stale cookie but the cream was still good.

Crumbs scattered over her legal pad. "What do you

know about writing a business plan?"

Cora Anne sat cradling the china teacup she'd always favored. "Nothing. Unless it's similar to writing a plan for historic preservation."

Hannah wrinkled her nose. That just sounded dusty. "Maybe."

"Why don't you ask Ben? Tennessee says he's really the brains behind all their business ventures."

Popping a whole cookie in her mouth, Hannah shrugged.

Cora Anne arched one brow. "You still have a thing for him, don't you?"

Swallowing shouldn't be so difficult. "Need milk." Her cousin waited, one arm hooked around the chair. Lips pursed like one of Nan's old barn cats stalking through the spartina grass.

Hannah guzzled a whole glass before facing her again. "There's no thing."

"Oh my gosh, yes, there is." Cora Anne clapped her hands together. "This will be perfect."

"Far from it." Hannah picked up her pencil. "And if I ask him it will only go to show how desperate I am to please my mother."

Cora Anne rolled her eyes. "Your mother knows how amazing you are. She's going to be happy you want to create a spinoff of the business."

"Or she'll tell me I'm still too young, too inexperienced, too immature—"

Her cousin grabbed her hand, stilling Hannah's ticking on her fingers. "You are none of those things, Hannah. Not anymore."

She curled her fist back into her lap, forcing a small smile and begging the quivers in her stomach to believe

Cora Anne's words.

Even though she hadn't gotten to the last of her list. Irresponsible. Not anymore.

She hoped.

Chapter Six

"Closing in January is not a bad idea." Gavin slid a dish of cheese grits Ben's way. He snagged the hot bowl and with the other hefted a basket of biscuits. The Sunday brunch rush was on, and the kitchen clamored with the sounds of cutlery and staff chatter. With the rattling of money made, not merely spent.

He hoped.

"Hold that thought, terrible as it is," he told his chef as he backed out the door.

The dining room was over half full, and the Baptist church wasn't out of service yet. Sunday brunch was becoming a local staple. He delivered the food and a smile to table eleven, where Mrs. Gloria Jenkins's hat announced her presence every week. Today's confection was all flowers and tiny birds, blue as the Sound. Man, he couldn't wait to get his boat out this afternoon.

Or tell Hannah about her Cousin Gloria's hat.

"We aren't closing. The locals love us." Back in the kitchen he grabbed a knife and sliced oranges for garnish.

"Not sure love will keep the lights on all winter." Gavin whisked eggs like a speedboat churned waves. Adding ingredients for the day's special—winter greens frittata—he continued, "Got to think about the bottom line, Ben."

"I think about nothing else."

"Then run the numbers." Gavin poured the mixture into a skillet. "You'll see what I mean. Even Charleston backs off in January."

Ben cubed a melon that had cost twice as much wholesale this week as they had all summer. Another reason they strived to keep the food local and seasonal, but fruit in the winter was a struggle.

"What about weekends only? Friday and Saturday dinner, Sunday brunch?"

Gavin shrugged, his lanky shoulders almost reaching the wide hoops in his ears. "You're the boss. But I wouldn't expect a big profit."

Ben pressed his hands to the counter, mentally calculating. Not liking even the fake numbers.

His sister breezed through the swinging doors. "Hey, bro, I know you're busy—"

"Got that right." He reached for a stack of ramekins and started adding fruit. "Why aren't you out front?"

"Hannah said she'd watch the station for me. Now listen—"

"Hannah's here?"

"Yes, and I know y'all have plans—"

"We don't have plans."

"Boat ride?"

"It's just business."

"Whatever."

"It's an all-business event week, Christy. Have you ever dealt with a wedding planner?"

His sister sucked in a sharp breath. "We eloped precisely for that reason."

Nearly six years and she was still defensive. He reached over her head, snagging fresh mint to garnish the fruit. "What do you need?"

"Just a couple hours without the kids. Please?" She took the mint from him. "Stop tearing the leaves." She grabbed scissors and snipped neatly, her fingers deft. "We haven't done any Christmas shopping, and Jared will be gone all week out to Arizona…"

His sister sure knew how to guilt someone.

He sighed. "Where's Mom?"

"Coming with us. She wants to buy for those Angel Tree families."

Great, now he seemed like the family Scrooge. Maybe babysitting would be his redemption. "Fine."

Christy squealed. "Really?"

"Why'd you even ask if you thought I'd say no?"

"Thank you, thank you, thank you." She added mint to the last dish. "And done. Good plating is worth at least a couple hours, right, Gavin?"

"You know it." The chef winked at Christy and slid the frittata across the counter to Ben. "Get on that."

"I'll have Jared bring the kids over soon as the rush is done, okay?" But she backed out the kitchen door before Ben could respond.

He sliced and plated. So much for blue skies, blue waves, and blue eyes focused only on him. Ought to feel relieved. Not wilted as the frittata's greens.

***

If it weren't for the wind stirring Hannah's bangs, the day could've been summer perfect. Sapphire water glittered beneath a bowl of sky—blue as the pottery she'd suggested Ben use to serve The Hideaway's infamous cheese grits. But the wind had a bite to it that made Hannah zip her jacket to her chin.

So much for cute.

37

Ben, rummaging under the boat's seats for life jackets, turned and held out a stocking cap with a bass fish emblem. "You might need this too."

Not with the static it would cause her hair. "You think? Because—"

He jammed the cap over her ears. "Warm is better than cute." His fingers grazed her jaw. "But now you're both."

"Uncle Benny!" Up the dock, Elizabeth's shriek rivaled the seagulls' cries as they circled overhead, hoping for an afternoon snack.

So much for alone.

Her stomach had dropped—then settled when Ben told her about the change in plans. Helping his sister out might be more friends than business, but it sure didn't hurt the image.

Hannah Calhoun Events embodies the values of family and community.

She'd add that to the business plan. Christy had lots of connections in this and surrounding communities. Of course, so did Ben. Which is why they should be on friendly terms. Though his thumb still on her jaw felt more like flirting.

"Hey, kiddos." He let his hand fall and spun, changing into fun-uncle persona as he heaved the children on board, swinging them wildly by their arms.

"Ben, be careful, please." Christy stepped lightly into the boat by herself and immediately grabbed a life jacket for Colby.

"Me? I'm always careful." But he caught Hannah's eye over Elizabeth's bow—turquoise today—and winked.

Maybe she was the one who needed to be more careful.

"Listen, sweet things." Christy tugged on the kids' jackets. "Tight enough?" They bounced and nodded. "Y'all be good for Uncle Benny and Miss Hannah, okay?"

"Okay, Mommy." Elizabeth answered for both of them as she took her brother's hand and pulled him to a seat on the boat's bow.

Christy waved and left. Ben tipped his chin toward the front. "You want to sit with the kids? They always start there, last about five minutes, and then move to the back where there's less wind."

"Sounds good."

"Sounds like chaos, but I'm glad you're on board. Literally." His dimples charmed her, making her think things that definitely were *not* business.

She might need one of those life preservers for more than this boat ride.

***

One would think two hours on the water with a half-dozen dolphin sightings and as many fruit snacks would wear a couple preschoolers out.

But nope. His niece and nephew made a beeline up the dock, one clinging to each of Hannah's hands, rattling on about the playground and ice cream.

"I think it's a little chilly for ice cream." Hannah expertly buckled Colby into the seat Christy had left in Ben's truck. Either she had a knack for kids or car seats were one of those things women knew how to handle. Pretty sure he'd be called sexist for thinking *that*.

Not sure what she'd call him for thinking she looked better than he'd ever expected. Tufts of her blond hair escaped his old hat, and her cheeks were holly-berry red. From the wind, surely.

39

"Can we slide? And Uncle Benny can push the swings?" Elizabeth leaned out of her seat and tugged his collar.

He submitted to the bear hug, and then tickled her belly so she'd let go. "Now swings we can do."

The tiny playground across from the Piggly Wiggly only occupied the kids long enough for Hannah to pull that stocking cap off and fluff her hair. He pushed Colby but watched her. She was never rumpled. A hair out of place no doubt drove her crazy.

All the more reason she wouldn't be interested in all the things out of place in his life. Like the voicemail on his phone he'd been ignoring for two days.

A family of bicyclists rode by, the dad towing a big-wheeled cart behind him. "That looks fun." Elizabeth launched herself from the swing. Luckily Hannah caught her before she could land in a heap.

"Careful, sweetie. You shouldn't jump unless you tell someone." Her eyes met his across the playground.

Ben swallowed and looked away. Bikes. Definitely less opportunity for jumping.

At the outfitters shop across the road, he rented two adult bikes with a tow cart attached to one. Hannah arched one of those perfectly manicured brows at him. "I hope that one's for you."

"Of course. Nothing I love better than hauling kids all over the island with the force of my muscles." He puffed out his chest and assumed a Superman pose that had Elizabeth and Colby clamoring up to hang off his arms. "Into the wagon you go." He settled them inside, fastened the harnesses, and then checked out Hannah.

She'd swung herself onto the old blue bike, long tested by hordes of vacationers, and waited with one foot anchoring her to the ground. "Ready?"

Maybe he could be. She'd released the zipper on her jacket enough that he could see the hollow of her throat contract when she swallowed and looked away. His gaze must've lingered too long.

"Let's go." He kicked off the ground and pushed the pedals, the added weight of the wagon less restricting than he'd imagined. Probably a good thing he'd been running more lately. That and Corona were about the only things that kept him sane at Christmas.

Hannah whizzed past.

"Show off." Ben called as she held up her hands, pedaling easily.

"Don't hate." She tossed the words and a sunny smile over her shoulder, and he wobbled a bit. Laughing, she circled back beside him. "We can take turns."

"A gentleman never lets the lady do the manual labor."

"Southern Charm 101?"

"Jeanne Townsend 101."

She leaned back, hands free again. "Your mom is really nice. She brought the triplets extra biscuits at brunch today so they wouldn't have to rock-paper-scissors for the last one."

"Yeah, she knows about feeding hungry kids." He meant the words in jest but felt his eye twitch all the same. Before his mother remarried, hunger had been a part of their regular life. Not something Hannah, with her perfect nuclear upbringing, had probably ever known.

"Speaking of hungry kids..." She darted a glance backward, bringing her bike dangerously close to his. "Think we need to feed them?"

"Christy says, if I eat, so do they. And after this

workout"—he heaved forward—"I'm going to require pizza."

"Pizza?"

Still close enough, he could see the wrinkle form between her eyes. "And lots of it." Surely she wasn't one of those low-carb girls.

"In that case, I better pedal faster." She left him behind again, but her laughter sounded like jingle bells on the wind. Like Christmas and happily ever after and things he knew nothing about.

***

"Can I ask you a question?" Hannah wiped Colby's saucy hands and kept her voice light. No reason for Ben to think she needed his help.

"Guess so." He added another slice to his plate. The way Ben put away pizza made her wish she could eat without worrying her skirts wouldn't zip.

"Cora Anne said you're good at writing business plans."

"That's not a question." He handed Elizabeth the piece of pepperoni she was trying to tug off his piece. "Here you go, kiddo. Now hands to yourself."

Elizabeth licked the pepperoni with only the tip of her tongue. Then, poking the whole thing in her mouth, she announced, "I like it!"

"Good. Your mom will be glad to know I rescued you from the blandness of cheese pizza." Ben winked at Hannah. "We'll add that to our short list of commonalities."

Edisto. Pizza. Business. Those things might be enough for a friendship but definitely not more. And thank goodness, because she needed to concentrate on building her career, not a relationship...

She sighed and helped Colby with his straw.

"Hannah? You had a question?"

"Oh, right." She tucked her hands in her lap, where he couldn't see her picking at her paper napkin. "Do you think I could have you take a look at my business plan and give me some feedback?"

"Yours or your mom's?"

"Mine. I'm thinking about going out on my own."

He frowned. "You don't like planning weddings?"

His narrowed eyes seemed out of place for the jovial bachelor uncle. This was a glimpse at the businessman, and she squared her shoulders. If she wavered in front of Benjamin Townsend, she'd never be able to face her own mother.

"No, I do. It's just—I might want to do something more than that. Or less." She swallowed and felt her throat burn. She would not cry. "It's like this—Mom and I don't always see things the same way. I like smaller events—like what we're doing with the Barron wedding."

He passed the rest of his pizza to Elizabeth and wiped his own fingers slowly, all the while keeping his eyes on hers. In her lap, her hands fisted, nails biting into palms. Just business.

But no one, not even Cora Anne, had listened to her with this kind of attention. "Anyway, I'd like to work up a proposal to show her, so she gets why I think I'm ready to do this on my own."

"And because you'll need funding."

"Right." She hadn't really thought that much about the fiscal side of things.

He propped his elbows on the table, resting his chin on steepled fingers. "It's a tough time to be starting a business."

"Really? Because you—"

"Tennessee and I are liquidating some assets."

Forget eating without worry. Now her stomach felt heavy, the weight of his words—and trust—more than she wanted. She'd known Ben long enough to get his business was his life.

"We got a tip that the real estate bubble might burst, and we don't want to go down with it. Why I like the idea of weddings. If we become a venue for you—or your mom—that's a steady income stream that could keep The Hideaway and the remodel business afloat."

So he did need her. To save his investments. No wonder he'd made good on the promise of a boat ride—and then been all the more willing to trade that potential date for an afternoon of babysitting.

"Hannah?" Elizabeth tugged on her arm.

The scattering of freckles across the little girl's nose was endearing. Someday she wanted to look down and see her own child, sun-kissed from the wind, a smear of pizza sauce on her lip.

"Can I have your pep'roni?"

"Sure, baby." She slid the plate across the table, keeping her smile—and her hope—firmly in check. Ben needed her just as much as she needed him. Nothing personal, just business.

Chapter Seven

He was dropping Hannah at the marina for her car when Christy called.

"Hey, I'm sorry we're not back yet. Traffic's worse than Spoleto." His sister knew how to exaggerate. No way there were more people downtown Christmas shopping than attended the annual summer art festival.

"Guess that means I'm on duty for another hour."

"Or two." He heard no regret in his sister's voice.

Rolling down his window, he called to Hannah before she could get in her car. "Christy says they're running late. I'm going to take the kids home. Any chance you aren't tired of us yet? My sister swears they'll go to sleep soon."

She lifted a half-smile at him and shook her head. His stomach plummeted—but then she said, "I'll follow you."

Regret twisted at him on the drive. Shouldn't have burst Hannah's idealistic bubble. He remembered those early days, when ideas were fresh and his pencil couldn't streak across a page fast enough to capture them all.

Should've just said he'd look at the plan. Since when had he become a realist? He halted his truck in front of Jared and Christy's quaint bungalow. Behind him, Hannah parked and exited quickly. She got the kids unbuckled, and he let them into his sister's house.

"What a sweet place." Hannah lowered Colby to the floor. Five minutes ago in the car, the kids had been asleep. Now they ran around the den, shouting at things Hannah should look at. Ben grabbed the cord for the tree's lights before Colby electrocuted himself. When Ben plugged it in, bulbs lit up the small fir tree, covered over in the kids' handmade ornaments.

"Look, Hannah. This is our fam'ly." Elizabeth proudly held up a family canvas that had been propped on a bookshelf. Christy had hung a "___ Days Until Christmas" sign in the picture's usual spot. A swirly 14 was chalked in the blank.

How different they were—his sister counted down Christmas's arrival. He counted toward its end.

Hannah took the canvas and lightly ran her fingers over the faces. "Family is a wonderful thing to have, isn't it?"

The photo shoot had been their Mother's Day gift last year. Their mother had wept when the prints came in, the seven of them—Christy's family, Ben, her, and their stepdad Lenny—all in white shirts and blue jeans against a backdrop of sea oats. Perfect all-American family.

At least in pictures.

Right on cue, the phone in his pocket buzzed. A Charleston number he recognized—and ignored.

Elizabeth ran off to fetch her favorite stuffed bear, and the clatter from the bedroom indicated Colby had just dumped out all his wooden blocks. Like he did every time Ben came over. Hazard of one time spending an hour on his knees building the kid a village. And people thought two-year-olds had short-term memories.

A different clamor sounded outside. Thunder rolling in. Elizabeth, now standing on the couch clutching her bear for Hannah's inspection, squealed.

"Baby, it's okay. Just a little storm." Hannah held out her arms, and his niece leapt into them. This time, when her eyes met his over Elizabeth's head, he didn't have the urge to make the moment light. He held her gaze, hoping she'd sense repentance.

Hannah eased Elizabeth to the floor. "Show me your room?" Hannah had an easy way with the kids, not a trait he'd have expected from someone who'd had so little interaction with them.

"I'll check on Colby, too." He crossed as they did, catching her elbow before they could collide in the small hallway. "Christy said maybe we could get them ready for bed?" He had no idea how to do that.

She glanced away, focusing her gaze on the painting in the hall. Botany Bay's sentinel tree, bare bones of limbs against an inky purple sky. He'd promised to take her out there, too.

"Sure." Hannah pulled her arm, once again leaving space between them. "Baths?"

His face must've betrayed him because she threw her head back and laughed. Barely a half-hour without that sound of merriment and he'd missed it. "Ben, surely you've bathed them before?"

"Does swimming count?"

"Oh, good heavens." She rolled her eyes and the heaviness between them evaporated. "Does Christy ever let you watch them this long?"

"I think you're a bad influence on her judgment." He grinned at her, teasing out a smile in return. One that made her mouth as enticing as the ice cream they'd refused the kids earlier.

Another clap of thunder sounded outside, and

Elizabeth yelped again. Hannah squeezed her fingers. "I promise it's going to be okay."

But as he crossed behind her to Colby's room, Ben wasn't so sure. He helped his nephew clean up the blocks—appeasing him with one quick tower the kid dropped with a neat kick. Ben pinched his toes, and then pretended to wrestle him so he could get him out of his shoes and clothes. "How about soccer instead of golf, little man? It's way more exciting."

"Says the man who's been known to fish all day." Hannah peeped around the doorframe, Elizabeth behind her. "Sissy here says no baths in a thunderstorm, so you're off the hook."

"You mean *we're* off the hook." He moved past her in the doorway, deliberately letting their bodies brush. Yes, definitely more than static electricity in the air. He felt reckless, daring, with a sudden desire to sit with her on a porch and watch the storm roll in over the marshes.

"Uncle Benny."

Luckily there was reality.

"Yes, ma'am?" He squatted to Elizabeth's eye level.

"Mommy always gets the candles ready when there's a storm."

"On it."

Hannah followed him back into the den, Colby now on her hip. "Do they lose electricity out here a lot?"

"Island living at its finest." He found the matches and started lighting the myriad of candles Christy kept around the room. She must've switched to Christmas scents because vanilla mingled with cinnamon and the heady smell of a pine forest.

Hannah found the kids' pajamas, and the four of them settled on the couch to read yet another *Llama*

Llama book. Every time Ben came over, seemed there was a new one of those. But he'd never heard the stories read in Hannah's rhythmic voice, the cadence of the rhymes rising and falling with the breaths she took.

He'd have listened to every single book on the shelf just to keep her reading.

"Ben?" The lilt dropped and, under it, he thought he detected exasperation. "Did you zone out with the kids?"

On either side of her, his niece and nephew snuggled. Colby's thumb dangled from his mouth, and he already snored softly. Elizabeth's eyes drooped, each blink longer than the last. Ben wanted to tell her he'd been caught in the magic of the moment—but that would sound romantic and ridiculous. Like something Tennessee told Cora Anne, no doubt. The scented candles must be getting to him.

He crooked his arms beneath Elizabeth, lifting her easily, though she was now forty pounds of deadweight. "Guess we should get them to bed, huh?"

Hannah's mouth had opened slightly—probably she'd been about to make another sarcastic comment since he seemed to bring those out in her. But she snapped her jaw shut with a little shake of her head. "Sure. Bed. Of course."

Yet her eyes lingered on his, long enough that he had to clear his throat before it dried completely. Definitely the candles.

They tucked the kids into their beds, and as if on cue, the house plunged into darkness. The thunder had rumbled over during their reading, followed by lashings of rain that beat the little house. But he'd been so caught up in Hannah, he hadn't heard the storm's tempo increasing.

Now he crossed to the front window and peered out. Total blackness, though a flash of lightning lit the pines in the yard, swaying in the wind.

"Goodness." Hannah stood at his shoulder, arms wrapped around her middle. "Hope they're not driving in this."

"They'll be all right. Jared's pretty smart, even if he does like golf."

Her soft chuckle pulled him away from the window. The candles cast a gentle glow all around the room, lighting the highlights of her hair, making her eyes sparkle. Hannah's idea of casual was designer jeans and a tailored blouse she'd kept hidden beneath her jacket all day. Now he could see how the cranberry-colored fabric draped her curves and complimented her skin's natural glow.

He stepped into the kitchen, needing some distance. "How about a glass of"—he opened the fridge—"milk?"

"Are there Christmas cookies to go with it?"

Ben peered in the snowman jar on the counter. "Yup. Grace Watson's famous snickerdoodles."

"Sounds great."

She went back to the sofa, settling casually, one leg tucked beneath the other. No heels today, he'd noticed. Those flat shoes that looked like a dancer's instead. He poured their milk into Christy's stemless wine glasses—the ones with the gold sparkles. Her fingertips grazed his as he handed over her drink.

More electricity.

More magic.

More reason he should sit in the armchair, but he chose the couch anyway. Propping his arm along its back, he watched her sip and sigh. "Good day after all?"

"You know, it really was." She beamed at him. "Those kids are precious."

"I think you mean precocious."

"No, I mean adorable." She leaned toward him, and his heart skittered. "Must be a family trait." Then she bit her lip, and Ben shut his eyes a fraction too long.

Just the candles. Just the moment. Just business.

But Hannah didn't look like business was on her mind.

***

She sat back. Had she really just said that? Called him adorable. Her mind backpedaled, and thank goodness, her mouth had learned to keep up. "I mean, because Colby looks like Christy, and she's got those sweet dimples. And Elizabeth's curls—"

Ben's hand on her knee dried up her torrent of words. "You want to talk about something else?"

Hannah exhaled. "Yes, please." She took a gulp of milk. *Calm down.* But her heart apparently wasn't listening.

"Tell me about the business idea."

Her shoulders relaxed. Business. Yes. That was still their connection. Putting her glass on the table, she straightened her spine and angled toward him, but only so she could watch his face as he listened. Ben might be a suave entrepreneur, but planning weddings had taught Hannah how to read even the most stoic of men.

"My thought is find the niche for small events—not inexpensive events, necessarily."

"Intimate." He nodded.

She tried not to hear any other connotation to that word. "Yes. I'm thinking swanky dinner parties, engagements, smaller weddings even. Especially second marriages. People don't usually go all out for those."

He rubbed the stubble on his chin, and though normally she disdained a five-o'clock shadow, on Ben it was attractive. Roguish. "That's good diversity. Will let you showcase your creativity."

She liked he thought that, even if it might not be true. "Maybe. Sometimes a great event needs to be exactly what the people say they want."

"Wants and needs are two different things." Along the back of the sofa, his arm warmed her shoulder through the thin fabric of her blouse. His voice dropped a bit, and she shifted closer.

"My mom and Lenny, they got married out at the state park." His quiet tone told her he was letting her into something sacred. "Just us, Tennessee and his mom, a couple close friends from church. We had Lowcountry boil for a reception, and Christy made the cake herself. Grace strung up all these lights and put flowers in mason jars."

Hannah could picture it. The sweetness and simplicity. "Sounds perfect."

"Yeah. Mom said she wanted a simple home wedding. No big fancy deal."

"Only you listened to what she wasn't saying."

"Right." Ben's arm had tucked her into his side now. Or she'd moved over. The mellowness of this simple evening had compromised her judgment.

This time, she didn't try to recover any space between them.

His fingers played with the ruffled sleeve of her shirt. "I read about a wedding that gave you all the credit. Big deal shindig out at Middleton."

Hannah tensed. "The Gibbes wedding?"

"Think so. Didn't tick all the usual boxes—you really must have understood that client."

At the time, she'd thought so. Far too much. She shrugged against his arm. What if he'd heard? "I tried. But really, sometimes, it's just a show. Weddings like your mom's? Those are usually the ones that stick."

"Well, Mom deserves that this go-round."

She didn't want to pry, but he'd never alluded to his father before. And she needed to change the subject. Leaning into him again, she whispered, "I'm sorry, Ben."

He stilled, his breathing quiet and slightly uneven. "You know?"

What she didn't know was how broken he may still be. "A little bit. I know he left."

"And why?"

Letting her eyes lock with his, she nodded. She wouldn't make him say something that had obviously cost him so much shame. Cora Anne had told her how Ben's father abandoned his family, letting a heroin addiction drive him away.

He exhaled, a whoosh of breath that seemed to deflate the cocky businessman he showed everyone else. "Broke my mother's heart. And ours." His chin tipped toward the canvas of his family. "But we don't need him. Never did, not really."

He set down his glass and linked his hands over his knees, leaving her longing for the warmth of his arm. So she placed her hand on the back of his neck, kneading gently, like she would for a friend under stress. She said softly, "It must have been terrible."

Surely he needed someone to talk to. She could be that. He had been for her, last summer, when her own grief seemed overshadowed by her cousin and all that had happened.

He kept his eyes from hers. "Guess you never worry about turning out like your parents, huh? They seem pretty together."

The sharpness in his voice made her hand drop. "They've had a fairly happy marriage, if that's what you mean."

"And happiness begets happiness, right?"

"Not always."

"You want my advice?"

"About business?" Because she was no longer sure she wanted anything else. His jaw had tensed, all sweetness gone.

"Keep the safety net, Hannah. Your mother is a curator of happily ever after, and from where I'm sitting, she's given you a pretty perfect life."

Hannah stood and picked up her glass. Her hands shook and she was afraid she would drop the glass, shattering it the way he'd just shattered their moment. "You know, Ben, my life might not be as perfect as you think."

"I just call it as I see it, Hannah."

"Well maybe you should take another look." She held his eyes, but this time heat didn't spark between them. She was tired of hanging on to her cultivated image, terrified to let anyone see its cracks. But evidently, Ben intended to keep his intact.

A car door slammed outside, just as the candle on the coffee table sputtered and died. Like the faint glimmer of hope she'd been harboring all day long.

Chapter Eight

Hannah arrived at the office early Monday morning, ready to put her weekend with Ben behind her, as readily as she did any other event.

"Good morning, sweetheart." Her mother sailed into the narrow conference room, coffee in one hand, a slim folder labeled *Jana Barron* in the other. "I've sent Emmie to deal with the linens, so it will just be us this morning."

"How was the Peyton wedding?" At first, she'd been stung when her mother suggested she take the weekend off and let Emmie handle the Saturday afternoon wedding at St. Michael's with a simple garden reception of cake and champagne. Exactly the kind of event she wanted to cultivate into something special.

"Picture perfect. Our girl's really come along."

Our girl. Nice of her mother to acknowledge Hannah's hand in training Emmie, but the implication still hovered. That she wouldn't have been successful without her mother's guidance.

Maybe she wouldn't be. But maybe it was time to find out. She sat straighter and rested folded hands on the glossy tabletop. "Mom, I'd like to talk to you—"

The St. Michael's Cathedral bells tolled the hour—nine o'clock—just as the tiny chime over their office door rang.

"Good morning, ladies. I heard y'all have a sweet tooth." Ben's voice sounded over the chimes. Three days ago, Hannah wouldn't have been able to read the nuances of his tone. But she heard it now, forced gaiety over a plea for forgiveness.

"Hold that thought." Her mother stepped out to the office's cozy reception area. "We're back here, Benjamin."

He sauntered in—no other word for it—with a white box. Flipping the lid with a flourish, he slid it across the table. Gourmet donuts decorated like Santa.

She looked from the red and white frosting back to him. "Where did you get these?"

"I have connections."

Of course he did. She also knew he'd probably had to leave the island before seven to deal with traffic and have time to pick up donuts downtown.

"Listen, Hannah…" He looked so earnest—like Elizabeth asking for pepperoni—that she couldn't help but smile.

"Aren't those adorable?" Her mother's return reminded Hannah this was work, not a social call. But when she snagged the folder off the table, her mother's neat stack of papers scattered out. "Do I need to get you some coffee so you're ready to finalize these details without making a mess?" Mom waved her own mug. "Lots of work to do."

"I'll get my own, thanks." Any excuse to step away and catch her breath. Not that Benjamin Townsend made her lose it.

But he followed her to the break room. "I'm guessing you didn't realize I'm sitting in on this meeting?"

"Nope." Hannah poured coffee that smelled like pralines. Emmie had been bringing in different blends all season long. Thank goodness the pumpkin spice was done.

"I'm sorry I upset you the other night."

The words were soft and small in her ear. He'd pressed a hand to her waist and leaned in close. Flutters quickened in her belly, and she closed her eyes hoping to force down this ridiculous response before a blush reached her cheeks and drew a comment from her mother. "It's fine, Ben." She stepped away from him, cradling her cup and avoiding his gaze. "Let's just make sure we're eye-to-eye for this event, all right?"

He moved back into her space, hot coffee the barrier between them. "You'll have to look at me then."

Pressing her lips into a thin line, she met his gaze. Dark, turbulent eyes that had experienced a hurt she couldn't fathom—and yet, there were times she looked in the mirror and saw that same yearning.

"Are y'all coming back or should I plan this event all by myself?" Her mother was using her vendor-friendly voice, but a hint of impatience seeped through.

As Hannah and Ben settled themselves at the table, her mother passed out the first draft of the Barrons' schedule, which began on Friday night with the rehearsal dinner at the groom's family home on South Broad.

Ben sat quietly through the breakdown of the rehearsal, but Hannah saw him tug more than once at the collar of his shirt. Probably thankful he was off the hook on Friday for nothing more than the forty-five minutes scheduled to rehearse the ceremony on the dock. They finally finished the two pages of rehearsal notes, her mother's and her copies scribbled over with additional reminders, and moved to the first page labeled THE BIG DAY.

Ben flipped ahead, counting. Hannah didn't mean to watch his lips move silently but she couldn't seem to look away. He sat back, tapping his pencil against the packet. "Ten pages."

Her mother nodded. "Lots to cover."

Hannah caught his eye. She couldn't resist the *told you so* smirk she knew she had. When her mother cast her attention back to the schedule and launched into discussing the hair stylists, Ben winked as if to say, *got this*. Hannah rolled her eyes. He had no idea.

Right on cue, the phone rang. Her mother swiveled and lifted the receiver in one fluid motion. Hannah cupped her mouth and whispered, "That will be the photographer calling to change his time."

"No, Marcus, we agreed. Three p.m. ... I'm sure the light will be fine. It's December. The sun sets earlier ... Marcus, we can't shoot an eight-person bridal party in less than an hour before the ceremony." Mom's breath whooshed out and with it her gentility. "Three o'clock or I'm taking you off my preferred list."

Ben stopped tapping his pencil when he heard the change in her tone. Hannah hid a grin behind her hand. Carolina Calhoun might have a reputation on Edisto as the softer of the Coultrie sisters, but those people hadn't seen her in action.

"All right, then. We will work with what we have, but that party will be off that dock no later than 4:15. Understood?"

Hannah winced. The ceremony was scheduled for five. They'd have guests arriving by 4:15. Which meant she or Emmie or one of the weekend's hired help would be on bouncer duty.

"Benjamin." Her mother set the phone back in its cradle, voice still hard. "Do you think we could open the hot chocolate bar on the front porch in order to keep early arrivals out of the photography session? Some people think only of themselves."

Hannah drew a mental line through Marcus Devereux's name on their list of vendors as she made adjustments to the schedule. They would use him if a bride requested, but he'd lost Carolina's recommendation. And they'd lost a half hour of margin desperately needed on a wedding day.

Across the table, Ben's Adam's apple bobbed as he swallowed. No doubt he'd just realized her mother epitomized what they'd been telling each other weekend. All business. Nothing personal.

Hannah straightened her spine. Her mom was right. She might still have a thing or two to learn.

***

Carolina tossed that photographer as easily as Ben would have tossed back a small catch. He had no doubt she'd do the same to The Hideaway if he failed to meet her expectations. He had to admire the simple professionalism, even as it had his palms sweating.

Already his business couldn't afford to lose hers. The venue deposit alone had more than made up for the revenue they'd lose closing for one night.

They were halfway through the list—6 p.m. Cocktails—when the office's front door chimed. A honeyed mix of syllables and greetings floated back. A moment later the intern, whose name he'd already forgotten but better relearn, appeared in the doorway. "Carolina, the Barrons are here."

Hannah tossed her mother a desperate glance as they rose and welcomed the clients. The bride had red-rimmed eyes. Before Ben could figure out the situation—

clearly this boded trouble—he was swept into a cloud of perfume that made him long for the sulfur smell of pluff mud instead.

"Oh, wonderful. You're here, too." Mrs. Barron draped her coat over Ben's arm. "Ever since we had to switch to a more ... rustic venue"—she raked a glance over his pressed khakis and light sweater—"this wedding has become one snafu after another. Jana, sit right down and tell Carolina what all we've had to deal with." She fanned her throat as she sank into Ben's chair.

Carolina, who had pasted on a smile as if she had all the time in the world for last-minute changes to The Big Day, sat as well. "Emmie, would you get us some water, please?"

Ben took the only available seat left, next to Hannah, who folded her hands over her marked-up schedule. Clearly brides and mothers-of-brides did not need to know every detail.

Across the table, Jana twisted her rock of a ring. "I apologize for coming in unannounced, but we had an issue come up over the weekend."

"More like a disaster," her mother interjected. "But one must bow to the rules of good decorum, wouldn't you agree?"

Carolina's smile pinched. "Of course."

"We need to add more guests, please." Jana's words rushed out like a rising tide. Beside him Ben felt Hannah's entire body draw up, taut as a fishing line.

"How many?" Carolina didn't falter.

Jana looked down at the fingers she'd now twisted together. "At least fifty."

Hannah turned her gasp into a cough, and Ben poured her a glass of water from the pitcher Emmie had just set on the table. Going from 150 to 200 guests wouldn't be easy, but they'd had that happen on more than one occasion at the restaurant when large parties arrived without reservations. The trick, he told his servers, was to never stop smiling.

Carolina must've learned that too because she brought back her softened face and nodded. "Fifty. We can work with that." Her eyes shifted to Ben, and he knew she was telling, not asking. "If it's what you want."

"It's not what I want." Jana's voice pitched, and her mother passed her a tissue. "But my father had too much bourbon at the office Christmas party—" She jumped slightly, and Ben would've bet his beachfront property her mother had kicked her under the table. "I mean, my father thought it best to invite his entire office staff after all, and they've been calling all morning to get the information. I told Mother we could maybe send an email?"

"An email." Mrs. Barron sniffed as if the word itself were contaminated. "This is simply not how it's done. I know you know, Carolina."

"Well, these things happen." Carolina stood. "We'll take care of it. You should have no worries this week. That's our job, to worry for you. We will get some more invitations printed up this afternoon, and I'll have Hannah deliver them to Mr. Barron's office."

Ben cleared his throat.

"Yes?" Carolina tilted her head, and for a moment, Ben wished he'd waited to bring this up. But technically, he wasn't her employee. His and Gavin's reputations were on the line too.

"We can increase the list, no problem with occupancy, but this is a seated dinner with a choice of filet mignon or

salmon. That order has to be placed tomorrow at the latest."
Carolina narrowed her eyes, and he scrambled. "Though, I
might can sweet talk my vendors into Wednesday." But it
would have to be Wednesday morning. Early.

Jana sighed. "This is why I wanted a buffet."

Her mother's hand fluttered to her throat. "This is
not a backyard barbecue, Jana Marie. We want to give
you an elegant wedding—"

"Maybe I don't care." Jana's chair rocked as she stood.
"Maybe I wish we'd eloped after all."

Her mother's mouth gaped, and she struggled for
breath. "You—wouldn't—"

Ben poured Mrs. Barron more water, while Hannah
took Jana companionably by the arm. "Come on. Let's go
for a little walk, all right? Let them finish all the boring
details." Her voice crooned, much the same way Ben had
heard her speak to Colby and Elizabeth on Saturday night.

Hannah led Jana out. Mrs. Barron sipped her water
and fanned herself. "She didn't really mean it."

"Of course not." Carolina came around the table
and sat beside Mrs. Barron, taking the lady's hand and
patting it. Ben would have felt hemmed in.

But Mrs. Barron relaxed, her shoulders rounding
back as she regained control. "I knew Carolina Calhoun
could handle any crisis."

"We don't have crises. We have solutions." Carolina
quoted what Ben figured was a line from her own
mission statement. "Now when Hannah delivers the
invitations, I'll have her take a headcount for the dinner.
We'll include our phone number and give them twenty-
four hours to amend their choices. Then Ben will place
the order. He'll pad it a bit, no doubt." She didn't even
look up to confer with him.

He folded his arms. Gavin wasn't going to like this. But it couldn't be worse than the Saturday night they ran out of shrimp and grits. Well, just the shrimp. Grits were always plentiful.

Which ... he glanced over the menu again while Carolina continued to soothe the mother of the bride. They hadn't altered the original, but if they did, it would free up a lot of hands for serving, now that there were extra plates.

"Now, you go on down to the salon and get that Monday massage I told you that you'd need, and we will take care of everything here." Carolina helped Mrs. Barron to her feet. Ben stood as well. He'd wait for Hannah to offer his next suggestion.

See how well they could really make the business side of things work after all.

***

"...thirteen, fourteen, fifteen. There." Hannah slid the last round of table drapes, neatly encased in plastic dry-cleaning bags on metal hangers, toward Ben.

"Told you I'd be good for the heavy lifting." He heaved the stack of linens and laid them smoothly across the top of the cart. In the storage room, gathering the first round of supplies for the Barron wedding, the air was close and hot. Or maybe she only imagined that every time Ben stood next to her in the cramped space.

She moved away from him now, putting at least two feet between them as she collected glass centerpieces the florist would fill with an exotic array of tropical flowers.

"Well, these will make a statement, huh?" Ben took the first vase she passed him. He held his hand up, estimating the height with flowers.

"The MOB wanted statement pieces." Ostentatious was the statement Hannah thought she was making. "Jana liked those." She pointed to the white ceramic wrapped in twine.

"Suits the venue better." Ben grinned. "Want to swap?"

"And risk my job and my life?" He clearly didn't understand who was really in charge around here.

"Speaking of swapping…" He knelt, arranging the glass vases neatly in the box as she handed them over. "I was thinking we could change the menu."

She fumbled and nearly dropped a vase. "Are you crazy? Or oxygen-deprived in this small space?" Had he not heard her mother with Marcus?

He stood, reached for the vase, and wrapped his hands over hers. "If I'm lightheaded, it's all your fault."

She closed her eyes just long enough to savor the touch of his hands over hers. "Why?"

"Because you fed me salad for lunch."

To avoid the glint in his eyes, she kept hers fixed on a point just above his head. "Carolina Calhoun events are planned, timed, and executed based on decisions made well in advance."

"In the restaurant world, five days is pretty advance."

"In the wedding world, it's a nightmare." She pulled free, just as her mother breezed into the storage room.

"Hannah, did we have enough linens?"

"Yes, ma'am."

But she flipped through them herself, counting. Hannah resisted the urge to roll her eyes. Mom straightened. "I don't know if these centerpieces will work after all, but there's no time for any more changes. Ben, can you finish loading this? I need Hannah for a bit."

"Of course."

Hannah followed her mother to her office and shut the door when her mother indicated. What had she done now?

Mom lifted a box of invitations from her desk. "The printer sent these over, so you need to go to Mr. Barron's office and distribute."

"All right."

But her mother still assessed her, eyes wary. "What's going on with you and Ben?"

Telling her mother anything would only make her worry yet another event was getting too personal. "Nothing. We're friends."

"But can you maintain a professional relationship?"

Hannah winced. "I've learned my lesson."

"I hope so." Her mother picked up the portfolio this time. "Because I'm turning the Barron wedding over to you."

"What?" She took the folder and all its contents— including her mother's notes already retyped from this morning. Her own still lay scattered across her desk. "Why would you do that at the last minute?"

"You were good with Jana. Cordial, but not friendly. You calm her, and she's obviously going to need that. Plus, your Aunt Lou is having a conniption over this Christmas Eve gathering. Wants everything to be like when Mama..." The hitch in her mother's voice passed before Hannah could offer any comfort. Before she could express how much she, too, missed her grandmother. Especially at Christmas.

"Anyway, the venue was your idea, and you've been doing all the work to set it up." Mom placed her hands on Hannah's shoulders. Squeezed lightly. "You've learned, and it's time I trust you again. Especially if you're serious about starting a partner business."

Hannah's throat thickened. *Finally.* "Are you saying you'll support me?"

"I'm saying I trust you to execute this event. Let's start there. Show me what you can do." Her mother brushed Hannah's bangs from her eyes, as if she were a child again. "I'd like to see your creativity and poise shine again."

"I won't disappoint you."

Mom shook her head. "I'd rather you don't disappoint the client."

When Hannah walked outside, headed to Barron Investments with the invitations under her arm, Ben was loading the company van. She leaned in the open back door. "You get a new ride?"

His grin melted the resolve she had to make her mother's trust a priority. "You want to hear my idea before I drive off in this beauty?" He patted the van's door affectionately. "Maybe I should trade in the truck. Start giving van tours of the island."

"That's your idea?" She knew it wasn't, but she could see him so vividly—a ball cap and a tacky T-shirt, telling tourists about the ghosts of Edisto's plantations.

"Nope." His tone shifted to serious, becoming the man who made decisions and believed in them enough to take the risks. Which is exactly what he proposed when he detailed a menu change.

"I don't know…" Hannah shifted the box in her arms. His proposal was better—easier even—than the planned sides. This menu would showcase The Hideaway's understated excellence. While reapplying her mascara, Jana had confessed she wished her wedding wouldn't be like everyone else's.

"Come on, Hannah. Let's be a little more inspired—suit the event to the locale. That's your ultimate goal when you're planning your own events, right?" The mischief in his smile and eyes had gone, and his words probed the part of her she'd tamped down in favor of reliable choices.

"I'll call Jana, and if she agrees, we'll do it."

"Yes!" He high-fived her.

She backpedaled away, quickly. "I've got to handle these invites. See you later." Touching Benjamin Townsend put her heart in dangerous territory, but conspiring with him might send her over the edge.

The problem was, Hannah missed that precipice.

The way she once held her breath to see if a bride loved the small—unplanned—touches she gave an event. The way it made her feel alive to hear a client's desires, all the while listening for their secret wish.

Clients thought Carolina Calhoun events were successful due to Carolina's ability to anticipate anything that might go wrong. Hannah, on the other hand, had always erred on the hope everything could be perfect.

Her heels clicked down the sidewalk as she remembered Ben's shoulder pressed against hers, and the way he'd laughed as she outpaced him on the bikes. She hadn't met anyone who understood her dreams the way he seemed to, and while she'd promised her mother she'd learned her lesson about mixing business and pleasure, maybe this time things would turn out different.

Besides, hoping for the best was a lot more fun than planning for the worst.

Chapter Nine

The wedding day dawned over the marsh—sky of gunmetal gray. Standing on his back deck, Ben shoved his cell in his back pocket. Three voicemails.

The man usually only left the one.

He hadn't listened to any of them. He knew what they'd say. *Hey, Benny, I need a little cash for the holidays. Got a job coming up after. I'll pay you back. Promise.*

Since the time his father started asking—Ben had been sixteen, working the shrimp boat with Lenny—he had responded immediately. Anything to keep that man away from the new life his mother had built.

Out of sight. Out of mind.

But every Christmas he crept back in, and every year, he asked for just a little more.

Ben leaned on the deck railing, stretching himself into the view that thrived on the lifting and lowering of the tides. When the water rushed in, one couldn't see the muck beneath the surface, the place where decay begat life.

Maybe it was time he left his father to claw his own way out of the mud.

***

"You." Gavin pointed his chef's knife at Ben's chest as he came through the swinging door. Steaming pots and swift hands blurred The Hideaway's kitchen from a place of steady activity into one of frenzied preparation.

"I didn't do it." Ben grabbed a coverall.

"Yes, you did." At the counter, Hannah stood beside Gavin, clipboard in hand, headset over her smooth hair. "Your idea to alter the menu."

"It's Parmesan grits and bacon-wrapped asparagus—"

"—with balsamic glaze—" inserted Gavin as he tested a lemon.

"—instead of fancy piped potatoes and green beans." He lifted a shoulder. They'd agreed. Well, he, Hannah, and the bride had agreed. Gavin said *fine*, and usually Ben knew better than to listen to that word. "These are our specialties. What's the big deal?"

Gavin's knife slit a lemon with precision. "You tell him."

Hannah flipped her bangs, and Ben noticed the shadows beneath her eyes. She'd been sending him texts and emails all hours of the night the whole week long. Girl needed this wedding to be done so she could get some rest.

"We're down two servers." Her tone snapped him back. "That's the problem, and those famous grits of y'all's require constant supervision."

Ben bit the inside of his cheek. Laughing at her wasn't going to help. "Grits aren't toddlers."

She threw up her arms, nearly smacking his face with the clipboard. "Gavin says—"

Ben circled her wrist, gently lowering this weapon of a harried wedding planner. "Gavin exaggerates."

His chef raised the knife again. "Watch it."

"I'll stir the grits."

"Every five minutes?" Gavin jabbed toward the large

pot, mist curling from under its lid.

"Every five minutes."

"Fine." Hannah snatched Ben's phone from his hand.

"What are you doing?" For the briefest moment, he thought she would scroll through his call record and demand to know why he was ignoring that Charleston number.

"Setting your alarm."

"Like that won't get annoying."

She gave the phone back, and the tips of her manicured nails nipped his palm. "Then I guess you won't forget."

What he would remember was the way her lashes fluttered when she tried to maintain composure. Then she was gone, swinging through the doors, talking to air it seemed, though Emmie must be on the other end of that headset.

He stirred the grits. Chopped and massaged kale and shaved brussels sprouts for Gavin's legendary winter salad. They'd changed that as well. Who wanted spinach when one could have winter greens drizzled with citrus lime vinaigrette?

Morning blurred into afternoon, the kitchen frenzy kicked up, and Hannah whirred in and out like a summer storm, always bringing a new dilemma but, somehow, making Ben's air more breathable. The temperature had dropped. Could heaters be brought down to the dock for the ceremony? The silver coffee service needed polishing, because someone had left fingerprints all over the sugar bowl. The radar showed a green bubble advancing their way, but the hourly forecast said it wouldn't rain until after seven.

At that pronouncement, her voice hitched toward dangerous decibel levels. Ben took her arm and propelled her backward, into the freezer where the cold air made her gasp. "Calm down."

"It's. Going. To. Rain." Her breath came out in little puffs of white. "And my mother—"

"Is going to—what? Fire you because it's raining?"

She hid her face behind her clipboard.

He pried it away, laying it on a shelf beside the prepared trays of cedar-planked salmon. "Hannah, you can't force everything to be perfect."

She dropped her head into the hollow of his throat, her shoulders quaking. He pulled her into the embrace without overthinking it—they were friends. Friends comforted one another. Of course he never hugged Tennessee in the freezer of the restaurant, but neither of them ever had epic meltdowns over wedding shenanigans.

"I don't usually lose it." Hannah's breath whispered under his collar. "My mother said…" She raised her head and stepped back, composure set again. "Mom said if I wanted to be a partner, she'd be supportive if I proved myself with this event. That's why she's staying away until later. She's testing me."

He kept his hands on her upper arms, cold beneath her thin sweater. "You'll pass. Hopefully we both will."

The furrow between her brows deepened, then relaxed. She put more space between them, retrieved her clipboard, and held out her hand. "Partners?"

He closed his fingers around hers. "Partners."

***

A gust of wind blew up Hannah's skirt, making her shiver and shift her balance on the stepladder.

"Don't fall," Emmie cautioned, holding out the last strand of lights.

"Got it." Hannah twisted the wires into place and hopped down. "Hit the switch."

Emmie flipped the button on the outdoor power strip Hannah had found in The Hideaway's storage closet. Tiny stars of light lit the underside of the tent. Emmie's smile stretched her cheeks. Hannah had never seen her so excited. "It's Christmas."

Hands on her hips, Hannah nodded. "Just perfect." They had planned for the setting sun and candles to be enough light for the late afternoon ceremony. But putting up the tent as a rain precaution meant something more was needed.

Something better after all.

The dock had transformed into a wedding wonderland. Lights twined around and under the tent and, strung from the flagpole, formed a tree of bulbs that glowed in the dimming twilight. All up and down Big Bay Creek, light strands lined docks and lit boats, some bulbs brightly colored, some classic white. The dark water glimmered with Christmas.

She'd forgotten how the homeowners here celebrated, and it had been just the inspiration she needed.

Ben was wrong. She could control everything within her jurisdiction. Weddings weren't just about setup and execution. They were about ambiance and attitude. That dark cloud might be hovering, but under this tent, the ceremony would feel like a Christmas fairytale.

She checked her watch. "Let's keep the lights off until after pictures are done. They should be here any time, then you ready the beverage service, and we'll have a wedding."

They'd added flavored coffee and Earl Grey tea to the hot chocolate station that was accented by glass bowls of all shapes and sizes, filled with peppermint and cinnamon sticks, chocolate shavings, and marshmallows. Spread out in tiers over a white tablecloth, the station was the closest thing to a snowy day Edisto had seen in a long time.

"This is my favorite part." Emmie sighed, looking out over the neat rows of white chairs, aisles adorned with candelabras and white lilies. "The anticipation."

"You'll make a good planner, then." Hannah slipped her heels back on. "I prefer when it's over, all tied up with a bow." Not entirely true, but she didn't want to share her favorite moment with Emmie. Anticipation— like hopefulness—sometimes let you down. Though ... she glanced over her shoulder at the work she'd done. Sometimes hope won.

In the kitchen, Hannah washed her hands and found an extra apron. She knew the fine line between coping and implosion when she saw it.

"Here." Ben pointed to a tray of salad plates. "Handful of greens, drizzle the dressing, arrange the oranges like this." His hands never stopped moving. She followed and hers picked up the pace quickly.

They worked well together.

For a few moments, Hannah lost herself in the repetition of activity, letting all the other worries push to the back of her mind. Then the kitchen door swung open, and the tension in the air crackled. Hannah sucked in a breath. She knew who must be standing there.

"What are you doing?" Her mother's soft voice would be less intimidating if it came out shrill.

"Helping."

Her mother stepped in further, the door closed behind her. "That's not the salad we ordered."

"No, ma'am." Ben jumped into the conversation

before Hannah could. "We talked it over with Jana and made some changes."

Her mother's eyes narrowed. "Hannah?"

"Jana wanted something more creative, and Gavin's kitchen runs better when he's working with his own recipes." She knew where her mother's thoughts were going—where they always went. "Nothing changed financially—actually, we may have saved a bit—and the bride is happier." She drew off the gloves she'd been wearing to plate the salad. "Pictures done?"

"What about the bride's mother? Shouldn't she have had a say?"

Hannah squared her shoulders. "This is my event. You gave me control. I'll handle Mrs. Barron." Though the thought made her stomach churn.

Her mother smiled—as if she knew a secret Hannah should have considered. "Yes, you will. Time to own the choices you make. I won't always be around to cover for you."

Ben glanced at Hannah, and she could feel the heat of the question he wanted to ask. But she didn't meet his gaze. Instead she focused on her future—stretched out before her, long and narrow as a wedding aisle.

***

Ben might not believe in miracles, but he was pretty sure this event came close. As the ceremony concluded, the inevitable rain drizzled down. But guests, huddled under large umbrellas as they came up the path, had no complaints when he greeted them at The Hideaway's front door. In fact, he heard more than one gasp of delight.

"Charming, isn't it?" This woman wore enough diamonds and pearls to likely pay his mortgage.

"Yes, ma'am. Table assignments are right over there." He indicated Hannah and the white-draped table of placards. "Y'all enjoy."

"Oh, we will. Do you know, perhaps"—she grasped her husband's elbow before he led them away—"if this restaurant is open year round? We much prefer the beach without the hordes."

Ben bit the inside of his cheek so his grin wouldn't be too wide. "This is my place, ma'am, and yes, we are open year round." Gavin would have a conniption, but his plan would work.

As Ben welcomed the last guests, the phone in his pocket buzzed. He slipped a look at the screen. Same Charleston number. Like it or not, he would have to deal with this soon.

Hannah appeared at his side. "Come with me."

He followed her outside, where the smell of rain and coffee mingled with her perfume. She looped her arms around his neck, and he set his hands at her waist.

"There." She stepped back. "Now I can let you know if we need anything on the floor." She'd set one of those headsets on him, in a move he'd do well not to read too much into.

"Here to serve." He smiled at her, hoping to coax back some of her teasing.

But she tossed her head and opened the door. "Let's go."

If it weren't for the buzzing in his ear, Ben would've assumed the event came off without a hitch. Mrs. Barron hadn't given her plate a second glance when he set it down, but not two minutes later, Hannah said, "MOB headed your way. I'll cut her off at the door."

He came out anyway. Might as well meet this

challenge head-on.

"Benjamin Townsend, what happened to my menu?"

"Just a few alterations, ma'am. I think you'll enjoy it."

"I will not." Her lips barely moved as she spoke. Ben glanced at Hannah. They'd expected irritation, but this was barely controlled anger.

He tried again. "Ma'am, your daughter asked for something different. We obliged."

"With no concern for guests who might be lactose intolerant? Like myself?"

Hannah's brows shot to her hairline. "Mrs. Barron, I'm so sorry. We were not aware of any allergies."

Mrs. Barron sniffed. "Of course not, because I chose a menu that wouldn't interfere. My daughter has been far too occupied lately to consider my recent health … concerns." For a moment the mask she always wore slipped, and Ben glimpsed a woman who was tired, and he remembered his mother. She'd had to make all the decisions, too. Sometimes, when he challenged those choices, she crumbled. Because he couldn't understand all the weight she carried.

He had to make this right.

"Ma'am, I will fix you something else. Anything else you want. And you're going to leave with a credit here at The Hideaway so after all this is over, and you just want to go out to dinner with your husband and relax, you can. I'll include a bottle of our best wine as well, and we will customize the menu for you when you return."

She lifted her chin in a small nod, but her eyes narrowed on Hannah. "What about you? This should not have happened at an event I'm paying you to coordinate." Shaky anger returned to her voice. "Alma

Gibbes warned me to keep an eye on you, young lady, but I trusted your mother so explicitly I didn't think it necessary."

Hannah's face paled and her eyes darkened. For a moment, Ben thought she might snap. "My mother had nothing to do with my decisions." Then, she dropped her eyes. "This should not have happened, and I offer you my sincerest apologies."

"I suppose that will have to do. For now." Mrs. Barron strode away, her composure slipping back into that mother-of-the-bride role.

His questions would have to wait. He ducked back into the kitchen with Hannah behind him. "Hey, Gavin, can you roast some potatoes real quick? We've got dairy issues."

Gavin, who had his feet propped up on boxes in the corner, taking the only break he'd had all day, frowned. "Should've known about those."

"Well if Ben here hadn't bulldozed his way into my event, we might have."

"What?" He spun to face Hannah.

"There was nothing wrong with the original menu."

"It was as cliché as all the rest of this nonsense." He'd gone too far. Knew it as soon as the words left his mouth.

Hannah sucked in a breath and, for a moment, reminded him of Mrs. Barron herself. "So what if it wasn't creative? The people paying for everything were happy."

"You said this was better—it would showcase all we are good at doing."

"Exactly." She folded her arms, color flooding her cheeks. "All *you* are good at with no regard for me. That's my neck on the line."

"Of course. And we're just your hired help." He walked away from her, wondering if, once she cooled off, there would still be any possibility—business or personal—hovering on their horizon.

Chapter Ten

H annah couldn't bear to see a look of disappointment on her mother's face tonight—not when everything else had gone so well. The bride beamed happiness and guests laughed over champagne and praised the food and décor and setting as though Hannah herself had made The Hideaway what it was.

"Mrs. Barron was not pleased, I take it?" Mom whispered through her smile as they distributed sparklers. A bright Edisto moon broke through the cloud cover, lighting the path lined with guests, now a little tipsy and a lot giddy.

Sparklers and alcohol really were a liability. She'd joke to Ben he should ready the fire extinguisher, but she wasn't speaking to him. Which made her feel like a petty middle-schooler, but right now, between her mother's fake smile and her own embarrassment, she really didn't care. Nor did her mother need a response to her rhetorical question.

"I'll get the lighters." Hannah left the porch. With everyone outside, the restaurant appeared relieved. Servers, shoulders slumped, cleared tables. Ben bussed the high tops around the dance floor, the corded muscles in his arms barely straining under the heavy weight of all those empty glasses.

Empty like all her grand plans. Offering nothing but a headache in the morning.

She squatted to root through the box of supplies carefully hidden beneath the placard table's cloth.

"Hannah?"

She jerked and the edge of the table caught her forehead. Wincing, she swallowed a squeal of pain as she stood. "Mrs. Barron."

"Are you all right?" For a moment the woman was a mother—and just that. She grazed Hannah's bangs back from her forehead, squinting at the bump. "You're going to hurt. Not bleeding though."

"I'll be fine." Her new mantra, stolen from Cora Anne who no longer needed the illusion.

Mrs. Barron tipped her head, studying Hannah the way she had scrutinized the flowers when choosing Jana's arrangements. "You do good work."

She did? Hannah tapped the lighter against her palm. "Thank you?" The lift on the end of her words escaped her control.

"My daughter is pleased, and though you may not believe me, making her happy is not an easy task."

Hannah liked Jana, but she had reason to believe this mother. She'd worked enough society weddings to know even the sweetest debutante could be difficult.

"Though I couldn't eat those famous grits, the guests enjoyed them. Immensely. Probably more so than if we'd gone with my choice." Once again, Mrs. Barron's gaze narrowed. "Though I would have preferred to be consulted."

"Yes, ma'am."

"Let's not have this happen again, shall we?"

Again?

"Despite rumors I've heard of your … impropriety…" Mrs. Barron raised her brows, and Hannah bit her lip.

"I'd like to hire you to coordinate a little dinner party for me in the spring. Jana's father has decided to retire, and we don't want a lot of fuss. Simple, but not…" Mrs. Barron's eyes tracked the restaurant. "Rustic. I hear you are quite good with such events?"

Perhaps she'd hit her head harder than she thought and was hallucinating. Her mother's voice crackled in her ear. "Hannah, we're ready for the lighters."

Nope, not hallucinating. "I can handle that, yes."

"Very well, then." Mrs. Barron smiled. The first true glimpse of joy Hannah had seen in her. "Can I tell you a secret?"

"Of course."

"I'm so glad this is over."

Hannah laughed, moving toward the porch. "So are we, since we start all over again on Monday."

"Do you ever tire of it?"

Hannah paused, glancing over her shoulder. Ben was heading back toward the kitchen, and his gaze collided with hers. She looked away. "No, not of the part that's happily ever after. Just sometimes of the work it takes to get there."

"And it is work." The older woman beamed as Jana came from the powder room where she'd been changing. "But if you have the right person, all will be worth it."

***

Ben cranked the dishwasher for the final load of glasses as Hannah came through the kitchen's swinging door. Gavin, swiping the last counter, tossed his rag in the hamper and looked between her and Ben. "I'm all done here, right?"

Ben folded his arms across his chest. "See you in the morning." Brunch would come too early, but he hadn't

83

cancelled. Didn't trust the profit margin without their regular Sunday crowd.

"The guests have all gone, and our crew has loaded up. I'm going to send them back to town." Hannah looked a little deflated, like a balloon when it skims the ground instead of floating high. "I'll stay and help you reset the tables for tomorrow.'"

"I'd appreciate that, but you don't have to."

"I want to." She leaned her shoulder into the door. "Turned out well, by the way. Mrs. Barron ... she was pleased."

"That's good to hear." He pushed off the counter and crossed the kitchen. Put his hand on the door she tried to exit. Ignored Gavin watching. "I'm sorry I was harsh. I'd really like us to make this a thing."

"A thing?" Her voice lowered, so soft he had to lean in and risk being near enough to kiss her. Which he might have done, if Gavin hadn't forgotten he wanted to leave. "I'm not sure if you mean business or something else, Ben." She pushed through the door, turned back. "But Mom was impressed. She'd like to talk to you about more events. I'll probably be sticking closer to Charleston for a while, building my portfolio."

Her words hollowed him. Events meant business. But he'd thought business meant Hannah. Working without her might not be worth the economic stability.

She rubbed her neck, and he felt the tension tightening his own. "I'll be out here. Brought you some new tablescapes. Our thank you for the frenzy that was this week."

Stiff as driftwood, he nodded. "Give me a few to finish up in here."

Back in the kitchen, Ben met Gavin's raised brows

with a shrug. His chef laughed. "Looks like you pulled off a winner after all. Just don't fumble in the end zone." He punched Ben lightly in the shoulder as he stepped out the back door.

While the dishwasher ran, Ben finally lifted the phone to his ear and listened to the voicemails. Needed something to take his mind off Hannah and the wound he'd caused.

"Hey ... son ... Ben. I know you probably think I'm calling for money ... but I'm not. I'd really like to talk to you. Please."

Phone connection must have been faulty because it sounded like his father's voice cracked on *please*. Ben deleted the voicemail and moved the glasses to a drying rack. Same song, different verse. Dad always said he didn't just need money. He wanted to see him, check how he was doing. But somehow, they never got around to talking about Ben.

***

Hannah tucked the waxy leaves of magnolias around glass bowls with floating votive candles, setting the tables for Sunday's brunch. How simple in contrast to the overpowering centerpieces Mrs. Barron had chosen. Might should have changed those, too, but no matter.

On the porch, Ben vacuumed cake crumbs. When he shut off the vacuum's low roar, Hannah heard the rain start again, a soft drumbeat on the tin roof.

"What's your favorite part?"

She looked up and found his gaze on her, even as he deftly wrapped the vacuum's cord. "Of what?"

"All this wedding nonsense."

Nonsense. She had no doubt he'd meant the word

earlier, but now he said it with a half-smile, as if trying to seep his way back into her good graces. She stepped onto the porch, setting the basket of leaves on a table. Jana and her new husband had circled the floor right here, a classic moment of belonging only to each other. That wasn't nonsense.

"My favorite part is the first dance."

"Really?" He'd lost his tie hours ago, and his collar hung open. Shirtsleeves rolled beneath his elbows. Hannah pulled on her lower lip. She could still feel the graze of his arm against hers as they plated the salads. And she could still hear the edge in his voice reminding her his stake in tonight mattered too.

She flicked her eyes away, over the dark marsh. "Really."

"I like the centerpieces you brought."

Mistletoe branches had been mixed in with the greenery, and the white of the berries glowed in the dim light, illuminating the tables and softening the room, blending it with its setting. "I hoped you would."

"Hannah…" The way he said her name. Almost a plea, as if he couldn't quite admit he might want something more than a business arrangement. "Come here."

He held out a hand and she took it. Let him draw her into the circle of his arms. "Let's dance."

"There's no music."

"Shh…" He bent his forehead to hers, a whisper of a touch that made her heart ricochet. But Ben's voice soothed, and his hand in the small of her back was warm. Familiar. "Close your eyes and listen."

She obeyed, even if only to keep from looking into the depths of his. The gentle lapping of the shore, the strumming of the rain, a simple melody she'd never heard.

Ben's arm slid around her waist, pulled her closer. She crooked her arm over his shoulder, leaning in. Letting him hold her and waltz her in slow steps around the porch. Her eyes stayed closed, and her heartbeat kept quiet time with the music of the night.

***

He'd promised himself he wouldn't do this. Wouldn't let himself get caught up in the romance of a late evening and the Christmas lights on Big Bay Creek and a job well done. But here he was, dancing with Hannah in the dimness.

It was as if she belonged here. She'd known without being told where every table went. Had brought magnolia leaves and mistletoe because that suited this setting far better than the greenhouse blooms he could get on the cheap.

She'd been in his head all evening, and not because of that headset. But because he'd made her cry. Even though she thought he hadn't seen. He had. He noticed everything she did and marveled at the grace. And maybe he ought to tell her. Maybe he ought to stop being afraid he could have his own happy ending.

He halted mid-turn.

She finally opened her eyes and looked into his with the only invitation he needed.

Dipping his chin, he grazed his lips against hers, and when she yielded, he pressed in. Tugging her against him, hip to hip, her body molded to his. In his belly, a flickering flame licked to life. He cupped her neck, tilting her head. Heard her soft moan as his lips broke contact with hers only to burrow into the hollow of her throat. He traced his way back to her mouth, where she tasted of wedding cake and peppermint and rain.

Their embrace worked in tandem. A push and pull of heat and desire, not unlike the ebb and flow of that creek rising outside with the tide and the rain and the pull of the moon, an ancient dance so many before them had known.

He hadn't known it would be like this. That kissing her would feel like home.

Like happily ever after.

When he let go so he could cradle her face, she whispered, "Don't stop." But he held back for a moment more, studying the depths of her blue eyes, seeing more than he'd ever bargained for at all the negotiation tables of his career. And what he saw was a chance to have it all.

A chance to work, side by side, with one person for the rest of his life.

He groaned and buried himself in the softness of her lips, her skin, her heart. So much for business. Hannah Calhoun had worked her magic on more than tonight's wedding. She had him believing he could be the man she wanted, the man he'd always wanted to be.

Chapter Eleven

Edisto might do everything else slow, but as far as Hannah was concerned, Christmas had come early.

On Sunday morning, she and Ben served brunch together at The Hideaway. He told Christy she could have the morning off, and Hannah played hostess, enjoying it far more than she'd expected. The restaurant peopled with distant relatives who talked to her about family connections as if she had the tree memorized. For once, she'd go to the family Christmas party and not wish for nametags.

After brunch, they went out on Ben's boat. Alone this time.

At first, he raced over the waves, chasing pods of dolphins and making her squeal like the kids had the weekend before. Had it only been a week?

Coming around Otter Island, he slowed the boat to a crawl and cut the engine. "Want to drift awhile?"

She wanted to drift right into him, to stay in this moment where everything was shiny and new as a present under the tree. He made her tingle all over—and he made her feel daring and adventurous.

More like the Hannah Calhoun she'd been before.

"You ever camp over there?" She peered toward the hidden depths of Otter's maritime forest.

"Where there's a rattler every five feet and the beach

is still littered with gun shells from World War II?" Ben stood behind her as she leaned over the boat railing. "Why not?"

Her laughter eased into a sigh as he wound his arms around her. "I like the seclusion."

"Here I thought I had you all figured out, and then you tell me you like camping." He turned her in his arms. "Hannah Calhoun, how will you surprise me next?"

She kissed him, sinking into a moment saturated with the salty tang of the sea. Pulling her closer, Ben kept her steady, even as the boat rocked and swayed beneath their feet.

They settled in a corner of the bench seat, her back against his chest, and she shared her ideas about upcoming events—and possibilities. "Oyster roasts are a popular rehearsal dinner or engagement party these days. Mom doesn't like to plan them because they make her miss her parents, but I think they're fun."

"We could definitely do some of those. Set up chairs around the dock? Light a big fire and stay out late… "

"Sounds perfect."

Ben shifted, and she fit even more snugly against him. "I think last night's wedding will really make people keep their eye on you. Much better than that other one Mrs. Barron mentioned."

"Think so, huh?" She should correct his assumptions about what Mrs. Barron had meant, but she couldn't think clearly, not with his breath tickling her neck.

"Really showcased your taste for … intimate events."

"Did it now?"

Warm against her jaw, his lips feathered light kisses to her hairline. "Definitely."

Hannah wanted to float away on this day, rather than

dredge up a story she wasn't ready to share. Surely by now she'd paid her penance for that wedding. Nora's—the bride's—brother, Todd, had simply been good-looking—and she'd been tipsy. Todd's kisses certainly hadn't made her want to sink into him and watch all the sunrises and sunsets of a lifetime from his arms.

Edisto's winter sun hovered behind Otter Island now, slipping below the tree line, leaving the air dusky. Ben disentangled himself from her. "Better start heading back."

She scooted into the seat's corner. There the warmth their bodies left behind seeped through her sweatshirt. Wind rippled through her hair, skipping along with the rhythm of boat over wave. Her stomach churned.

The after-party had been the real undoing of her reputation—and her mother's. Slipping away from her post-reception duties to do shots with Todd and the other groomsmen and bridesmaids culminated with the embarrassment of her mother finding her and Todd in the coat closet of the plantation. A mistake she'd regretted every day since.

Her cheeks burned despite the air's chill. She needed to come clean with Ben about why she ought to separate her name from her mother's business. The gossip hadn't been rampant, but it had a way of rearing its ugly head when she least expected. Like last night.

"You got awfully quiet." Ben boosted her onto the dock once he had the boat secured in its slip at the marina.

Down the creek, colored lights switched on, brightening her mood. How much had changed in the twenty-four hours since she'd switched on twinkle lights at The Hideaway's dock? "I was just thinking."

Cupping her cheeks, he bent his head to hers. "I sure hope it was only about me."

She pressed her lips against his in answer. Sure, she'd like nothing better than to only think of him from now on.

**

He hadn't seen Hannah in four days.

Longest four days of Ben's life. Today they were meeting a prospective client at The Hideaway—hoping to book one of those small but elegant parties Hannah wanted to make her niche.

He'd throw a party for anyone, so long as she was around. His house phone rang and he answered, even though it was probably a sales call.

Volunteer Fire Department. How many times could he give to them in one year? They were worth his donation though—except now he'd be a couple minutes late.

Ben opened his front door just as his father exited a dated sedan in the drive.

He stopped, twisting his palm against the door handle. His breathing hitched, but he caught himself as the scruffy man with stooped shoulders climbed his steps. "What are you doing here?"

His father paused, one step from the porch. "I called. Several times."

"I know."

"Why didn't you ever answer?"

Ben slammed the door behind him. "Why didn't you quit calling?"

His father spread his hands wide, as if offering surrender. "I don't need money."

"You always need money."

"Not this time. This time, I came to talk. That's all."

Ben glanced at his watch. "I'm late for an appointment."

"Please."

He looked at his dad. Probed the sight before him. The man's eyes were open, clear. Not red-veined, not drooping. And though he still looked undernourished, the hollows in his cheeks had filled out a bit. As if he'd had more than one square meal in the last few weeks. Ben sighed. "What do you need?"

"Forgiveness."

The answer was out of character for the man who once left red welts of belt marks across his legs. The man who tore their kitchen apart with his bare hands looking for Mom's cache of extra money so he could get a fix. The man who told Ben last year if he threw in an extra fifty, he wouldn't come back.

Ben moved to one of the rockers on the porch and sat. Waved a hand at the other. Dad kept to the chair's edge, as if afraid to relax against such support. "I've been working the twelve-step program at rehab."

Ben snorted. "That's a new one."

"Really." Dad sighed, and Ben could almost believe he sensed regret. "I messed up."

"That's putting it mildly."

"Ruined your life."

"Well..." Ben leaned forward, clasped his hands. Thought about Hannah and the way she believed in hope. "Truth is, it got better after you left. After Mom found Lenny. We made a real family."

He meant the words to sting, but when they hit their mark and Dad winced, Ben bit his lip. Hannah Calhoun took a chance on him, so maybe he should take a chance on this good-for-nothing shell of a man. The phone in his pocket buzzed. "I've got to go."

"Son, I've been told there is nothing more important than living each day right, even if you have to do it one day at a time." The way his father looked at him made Ben feel small again, as if he were six years old and Dad was reprimanding the way he pulled Christy's hair. "I told you I didn't need anything, but I do. I need this."

Ben wanted to leave. Wanted to fling his truck into drive and go to Hannah and plan happiness for other people, because he didn't like the package it came in for him. This broken-down man, how had he ever been a father?

"Forgiveness doesn't come wrapped like a present under the tree, Dad." His father's eyes misted as soon as Ben spoke the endearment. "I'm not sure I'm ready."

Dad nodded. "Can you try?"

Ben's keys cut into his fisted palm. Try. After fifteen years, this man wanted him to be the one who tried. His phone vibrated again. Hannah. "I'm leaving."

His father stood with him and grasped Ben's shoulder before he could move. "This time, I mean it, Ben. I won't come back asking you for anything, ever again. Your choice."

He jerked away. "How is that fair? None of this has ever been my choice." Pushing his father aside, Ben thundered down the porch steps to his truck. But the strangled sound of breath halted his stride.

He turned. On the porch, his father collapsed, clutching at his left arm. Gasping like a fish out of water.

Chapter Twelve

Hannah parked in the empty lot beside The Hideaway and checked her phone. No missed call from Ben indicating he'd be late. Her dashboard said 12:17, her watch said 12:20, but her phone said 12:15. So he wasn't late. Not yet. Not technically.

She might ought to let Cora Anne synchronize her clocks.

The walk-through with the Pinckneys was scheduled for one that afternoon, so they'd been good to give themselves this buffer. She stayed in her car, reviewing the event request.

Her first solo.

Squeezing in a consultation with this client just before the holiday had been difficult, but Mrs. Pinckney came on a recommendation from Mrs. Barron. They were looking for a place to renew their vows around Valentine's Day. The Hideaway had everything this couple wanted, and Hannah intended to deliver on anything else.

She called Ben, phone pressed between her ear and shoulder as she jotted a couple more suggestions on her notes. Straight to voicemail. Must be on his way.

She tapped her pencil against the menu request. Gavin would make this something more special than a choice of chicken or fish. People really had no imagination.

At 12:40—or thereabout—she walked the restaurant's

perimeter. Was he down at the dock and she'd overlooked the boat?

No. She called again. Voicemail. "Hey … it's me. You get caught behind a golf cart driving down Palmetto or something? Where are you?"

Just before one o'clock, a Lexus pulled in The Hideaway's drive. Hannah pasted on a smile and promised herself there was a logical explanation. He wouldn't flake out on her.

Or would he? Ben might know business, but he'd told her relationships required more work than he knew how to give. Maybe they shouldn't have tangled things after all.

"Good afternoon, Mr. and Mrs. Pinckney." She extended her hand to the well-dressed couple. "How was your drive?"

"Delightful. Every time we come out here I can feel time slow down." Mrs. Pinckney pushed back oversized sunglasses and beamed. "Thanks so much for working us in last minute."

Her husband took her hand. "Look at that creek, honey. Doesn't it make you want a boat?"

Laughter cascaded over the frayed edges of Hannah's nerves. Mrs. Pinckney hugged his arm and fell in step beside her husband. "You're determined that will be your anniversary present, aren't you?"

As they explored, Hannah snuck a glance at her phone. Nothing. She'd thought planning an event like this—for a couple who had made it the long haul to forty years—would be a sign for her and Ben.

Evidently she'd been wrong.

She walked the Pinckneys all around The Hideaway, extolling the virtues of wide porches, trying desperately not to panic. If Ben had left her a key, they'd go inside and she'd make an excuse. But she had nothing.

Tennessee's truck rumbled into the parking lot.

"Excuse me a minute." She dashed toward him.

"Hey, there." His long legs ate up the space between them, meeting her at the porch. "Ben called and said I should come let you in so you can show these fine people our humble establishment."

Hannah forced a smile—and widened her eyes at Tennessee. They may not yet be family, but he needed to learn to read this look. "Thanks so much. Ben's on his way, then?"

Tennessee strode up the steps, and Hannah's exasperation grew. This man never revealed anything he didn't think needed to be known. "He's caught up with a family issue, but he said you would know exactly what all to say."

She snagged his elbow as he stepped aside to let the couple enter. "What's wrong? Is it one of the kids? Was there an accident?"

Tennessee nudged her toward the door. "Take care of this, and then I'll fill you in. But he's ... fine. The kids are too."

"Well, I'm not." But she pivoted and went inside, putting on a smile wide enough to mask her frustration. "Let's talk about how we can set this up for y'all."

***

His father finally came to apologize and, instead, had a heart attack. Crouched in a hospital plastic chair, Ben massaged his temples. He still couldn't believe he was

97

sitting here, waiting on a doctor to tell him if his dad would live or die.

He didn't realize he still cared.

The elevator chimed, and a familiar set of heels clicked his way. *Hannah*. He raised his head and took her in—drinking in how clean she always looked. Fresh and un-rumpled, even though she'd given a tour of The Hideaway that, according to Tennessee's text, had included the dock, the green space, and the building's entire perimeter.

Ben always ironed his shirts, pressed his khakis, wiped the mud from his shoes. But he also knew it was a façade, that underneath a polished exterior he was a mess.

And Hannah deserved better.

"Hey." She perched in the chair beside his, reached for his hand. "You okay? Tennessee filled me in a little bit. Your dad?"

The barrage of questions snapped Ben back to reality. "Sorry I missed the appointment."

"Don't worry about it." But her voice trembled. He stood, needing the distance.

"Of course I'm worried. I need that contract."

She rose as well. "You mean *we* need that contract, right? Because this is a team effort."

"Yeah, whatever." He deliberately tracked his eyes away from hers, concentrating on the wall sign about washing hands to prevent spreading the flu. As if all it took was soap and water to wash away the invisible threat lurking around.

She reached out again. Squeezed her fingers around his elbow. "Tell me about your dad, Ben."

Pulling away, he sat. Casualness willed into his

stance. No big deal. No mess here. "He'll be fine. They're putting in a stent now. Once he's good, I'll head out."

"But what was he doing at your house?" Maybe she wasn't probing. Maybe she really wanted to understand.

But even he didn't have that luxury. "He comes over every year about this time. Needs money. I give it to him, and he goes away. Best for everyone if he stays far, far away."

"Does your mom know?"

He shifted. "She's got enough to worry about."

"So do you."

Now he swung around, faced her. "What are you doing here, Hannah?"

His tone shut her down—and he'd intended it to, but still, when her eyes widened, regret twisted his gut.

"Thought you could use a friend, that's all."

"There's no way you could ever even begin to understand what this is like." He didn't know why he chose that moment to lash out—why he chose her as his target. But seeing her in this place, in her heels and pearls, undid the knot in his gut. He'd held himself together for so long that when he finally let go, his emotions unspooled faster than a dropped fishing line. "Look at you, Hannah. You're perfect. Your life is perfect as Christmas—as fairy tale weddings."

She shrank away from him. "Is that what you really think?"

"The shoe fits."

"You're not the only one with an image to uphold, Ben Townsend." She stood and crossed to the window that overlooked the gray parking lot. Someone—some goodhearted nurse probably—had stuck holiday cling art all over the glass. Hannah traced a snowflake.

"That wedding everyone keeps bringing up? They don't remember it because I did a good job." She looked up and must have seen his hardened face in the reflection because she didn't turn around. "I was foolish enough to think the bride was my friend—and naïve enough to get caught in a compromising situation with her brother." Now she turned, stepped toward him. "So I know what it is to have everyone watching to see what you'll mess up next."

Ben unhinged his jaw and moved away from her. "You causing a stir at some high-falutin' wedding is hardly the same thing as this, but it's exactly what I'm talking about, Hannah. You have no idea what dysfunction really is."

"I guess I was wrong." She grabbed her purse. "About a lot of things."

She waited, and he knew she would stay if he asked. If he apologized. If he dropped his own show and put all his cards on the table. But he didn't want to find out what she'd do when this all became too much. If that wedding incident had undone her, how would she handle the embarrassment that had always been his father?

He'd already learned. The only way to avoid disappointment was to have no expectations of anyone but himself.

Chapter Thirteen

After four hours spent pressing a needle and grosgrain ribbon through dozens of pinecones and magnolia leaves, Hannah was certain her fingertips would never be the same. An excuse she used every time she thought about calling Ben.

Instead, she threw herself into the final preparations for the Christmas Eve party at the farmhouse. Traditionally, Nan always gathered family together for a simple meal—soup and cornbread had been the final years before the festivities halted after Granddaddy died. But her mother and Aunt Lou recalled less lean times, and they insisted on rekindling those with standing rib roast and Santa Claus, who would bear a sack full of gifts.

They also insisted on traditional décor, which accounted for Hannah's injured fingertips. Though she had to admit, once the homemade garland was looped around all the doorways and adorned the staircase, the painstaking hours had been worth the effort. Aunt Lou had gone so far as to take down the white curtains in the living room, replacing them with red ones she'd found in the attic. Mom's laughter had drawn both Hannah and Cora Anne from their post outside stringing more lights.

"Look girls." Her mother held up the simple drapes, colored as bright as holly berries. "Mama dyed these one Christmas. Now that's decorating commitment."

Cora Anne looked at Hannah and grimaced. "I'm

never dying my curtains for Christmas."

Hannah snagged her arm through her cousin's. "That's what Target's Christmas aisle is for."

"Do you think Target has a Santa we could borrow?"

At her aunt's question, Hannah stopped in the doorway. "Doubtful, Aunt Lou."

Mom lowered the curtains. "Are you telling me you didn't get a Santa?"

Aunt Lou sank onto the bottom of the stairs. "I don't know how I forgot. Especially since I love to check a list twice." Her wan smile and attempt at humor did nothing for her sister, who tossed the heap of red fabric onto the couch.

"Hannah, I told you we should've been in charge of this."

Aunt Lou rubbed her temples. "I'm sorry."

Her mother softened and joined Aunt Lou on the steps. "We'll figure it out. Right, Hannah?"

Somehow Hannah wasn't too sure about the *we* in that statement. "Of course." Two days before Christmas. Sure, finding a Santa wouldn't be a problem.

She trailed Cora Anne to the kitchen where her cousin called Tennessee from her cellphone, putting it on speaker so Hannah could hear.

"Lenny might do it." He filled them in on Ben's stepfather's Kris Kringle credentials. "He's grown out his beard, and he dressed up last year for Christy's kids, so I think he's got a suit. Just have to pad him, but that's what pillows are for, right? Get Ben to ask him."

Hannah bit her lip and refused to look at her cousin. Over the phone, Tennessee took only a second to understand her silence. "So this is why he's been in a bad mood."

Cora Anne raised her brows. Hannah winced, grateful Tennessee couldn't see this exchange. "I have nothing to do with that. Probably it's his dad."

"No, his dad's good. Out of the hospital, back at his rehab center. He and Ben are talking more than they have in fifteen years."

"Well, we're talking less, and that's probably for the best."

"Is this one of those don't-mix-business-and-personal lines you two keep throwing around?"

"Can you have Lenny call us, please?"

"Don't worry about it. One of us can ask him and let you know. But Hannah"—his tone shifted to serious—"Ben doesn't always say what he means."

She walked out of the kitchen, certain of one thing. Ben had meant exactly what he'd said—she couldn't understand his life, and after hearing about her own mistake, he wasn't interested in her trying.

***

Ben had never been a hunter, but he came out every Christmas Eve morning with Lenny. His stepfather's deer stand in the top of a tall poplar tree swayed a little in the December wind. Ben blew on his hands to warm them.

"So you'll do it then?" He kept his voice barely a whisper.

On the walk into the woods, he'd asked Lenny again about playing Santa at the Coultrie family's Christmas Eve gathering. But Lenny still hadn't given him a straight answer. Kept turning everything Ben said right around on him—asking how he really felt about what had happened with his father.

Interesting enough, Lenny had said nothing about how Ben's mother had reacted to the news Ben had been paying Dad to stay away. But he knew his mom would be up sipping coffee and flipping pancakes when they returned—those traditions again—and Ben knew she would want a word.

"Shhh…" Lenny's hushing came out under his breath. So soft Ben had to lean in to hear him. His stepdad pointed to the clearing. A doe stepped out, lightly, her hooves making no sound despite the fallen leaves.

Lenny raised his gun.

The doe swiveled her head. A quick jerk and a fawn emerged behind her. Must have been a late birth—the baby still bore the white markings of its youth. By this time of year most were big enough to have left their mothers.

Beside him, Lenny's breath whooshed out, and he lowered his gun. Quick like lightning, the two streaked across the clearing.

"Not gonna take a parent from a child." His stepfather clapped a hand on Ben's shoulder. "Seen enough of that to last me a lifetime."

"Can you just tell me if you'll play Santa so I can relay the message?"

Lenny cocked a brow. Reached in his pocket for a wad of deer jerky that he stuffed in his mouth. There had been a time the man had dipped tobacco, but he'd stopped when Ben's mother said there'd be no such substance in her house, ever again.

He offered the package to Ben, who sighed and took a piece. The chewy dried meat worked his jaw while he waited.

Finally, Lenny set the gun beside him, and linked his fingers together. Nearly praying. "I'll do it on one condition."

"What's that?"

"You call Hannah yourself and tell her."

Ben shifted, legs gone numb with cold. Wishing his heart could go numb, too. "She's mad at me."

"Hurt. That's different."

"Still won't make her answer her phone."

"Ben, I know you think, because of your dad, your life is one big tangle, too. But that's not true. We are who we choose to be." Lenny waved his hand at the woods. "Mercy is all around us—ingrained into us and everything in this world. Extending it doesn't make you weak. Holding it back does."

"I've talked to that man every day since he came."

"But have you listened?"

Ben sucked in a breath of frigid air. Had he? He'd heard the apology. The excuses. Yeah, he knew his father almost died on his front porch, but did he believe it mattered more that he'd almost died without Ben's forgiveness?

His breath heaved out. A puff of fog. He might not want it to, but it mattered.

"Speaking of listening…" Lenny leaned back against the tree trunk. At ease, now. A sign he was done with stalking the hunt for today. "That girl probably has a story you need to understand, too."

He snorted. "Hannah? She's had a pretty golden life."

Lenny swung his legs out, readying for the descent down the ladder. "Nah. Those are usually the ones most afraid of messing up."

Her face—the emotions that played over it in that

hospital window when she'd told him what she'd done—was still stuck in Ben's mind. Hannah's indiscretion might seem petty to him—especially in comparison—but that night had nearly ruined her. When he remembered the tone Mrs. Barron had originally used, the way the woman had treated Hannah with disdain from the moment Carolina handed over the wedding's reins, he knew he'd been wrong to dismiss her attempt at empathy.

Because she did understand what it was to fear failure.

"Slow down, son." Lenny grabbed his shoulder as they strode through the woods. "Your mama's not going to eat all the pancakes herself."

Ben wanted to run—all the way to Charleston if need be—and tell Hannah what he'd suddenly realized. Two people afraid of deserving happily ever after probably ought to work together.

But he slowed his steps to his stepfather's, the idea generator in his mind already humming. "Lenny, if you'll loan me your Santa suit, I'll make you a deal."

"You're pretty good at those."

His grin spread wide, despite his numb cheeks. "Let's hope you're not the only one who thinks so."

Chapter Fourteen

For the party, Hannah had bought a sparkly gold dress. She spun in front of her mirror, twirling in her flouncy skirt.

"Are you pretending to be six years old again?" Her mother stood, smiling, in the doorway of Hannah's basement apartment. Her hair swirled around her shoulders, and she'd traded her usual classic navy for a floor-sweeping dress the color of her favorite Merlot.

"Wow, Mom. You look stunning."

"Thank you, sweetheart." Mom crossed the room and tucked Hannah's bangs behind her ear. "So do you. Will we see Ben tonight?"

"I don't know." He'd called that afternoon, but she hadn't answered—and now she wondered if it was too late to try again. Maybe their magical moment was only that—a moment.

Her parents made light chatter on the drive, but Hannah sat in the back and watched the darkness swallow up the island the closer they got to the farm. Her dad hit the brakes a few times as whitetail deer bounded across the road.

The gates to the farmhouse lane were graced with magnolia wreaths and red bows, the motif carried throughout the farmhouse. Lights lit up the yard as family gathered on the porches, spilling over from inside.

"Did Aunt Lou invite the whole Jenkins and Coultrie tribes?"

"Of course not." Her mother sniffed. "Only the people we like."

Hannah laughed. "Then why is Cousin Gloria here?" The ample woman waddled to the front door.

"Because Mama would've invited her." Reason enough.

Inside, Hannah wove her way through the crowds. The house could have been a centerfold for *Southern Living*—in the sixties, since Aunt Lou still refused to update any of the furnishings.

Cora Anne waylaid her in the living room, a glass of their grandmother's famous Christmas punch in her hand. "Hey, has Ben found you?"

"No, and I doubt he's looking."

Her cousin furrowed her brow. "Now who's being stubborn about happy endings?"

Hannah folded her arms. "It's best if Ben and I stick to business, and since I'm not talking that tonight, we have nothing to say."

"Lenny's sick."

She gasped. "Okay, that's business. I promised Aunt Lou a Santa." Peering around the room, she didn't see Ben. "Where is he?"

Cora Anne shook her head. "I don't know. He said he'd handle it."

Great. Who knew what that meant? But from outside came the sound of jingle bells. Aunt Lou stepped into the living room and clapped her hands. "Children, guess who's here?" There were gasps and whoops.

"Guess he handled it." Cora Anne took Hannah's elbow and guided her to the porch where Santa Claus had settled himself in the swing.

"Ho, ho, ho. Have there been some good boys and girls on Edisto this year?" Santa, a bit lean despite the puffed pouch of belly, shook a canvas sack. "I've got a little something for anyone who's on the nice list."

As the children swarmed—even her triplet cousins were into presents despite being in middle school—Hannah elbowed through the crowd. Surely not—

"Ho, ho, ho. What do we have here?" Santa waggled his bushy brows at her. One was crookedly pasted on. "Such a pretty lady deserves a present, too." He held out a small box wrapped in bright red foil.

Hannah took it and leaned in. "I know it's you."

Ben puffed out his cheeks. "Santa is full of surprises tonight."

Thank you, she mouthed. He'd recognized this simple tradition's importance. And he'd met it, even if he did think Christmas was about as much nonsense as a big, showy wedding.

In the farmhouse foyer, Hannah tugged the paper off the box, wondering if he'd passed her the same trinket the kids were uncovering. Edisto key chains shaped like dolphins or sand dollars.

Sure enough, nestled inside the box was a gold key chain—a starfish. But attached to it was a key. Hannah turned it in her palm and realized a note was tucked inside the box. She pried it out, and Ben's bold script read, *This is the key to The Hideaway. Let's make some happily ever after.*

Tears rushed up her throat and pooled in her eyes. She swiped quickly, though runny mascara hardly seemed a problem tonight. Was she wrong to read a double meaning into his words?

"Ho, ho, ho. Now kids, who wants to help give Santa his Christmas wish?" Ben's voice boomed over the porch. Hannah leaned against the wall, a smile on her lips. That crazy man. What would he come up with next?

Suddenly a gaggle of giggling kids swarmed the foyer. "Hannah, Santa says you have to stand right here." One of her second cousin's daughters pushed Hannah to the center of the room as Ben came in the door.

"Thank you, kiddos. Santa says, go have cookies!"

She stayed rooted to the floor, watching him. He stood in front of her, and mirth flitted at the corner of his lips. "We need to talk."

"Right now?"

"Well … there's more than one way to apologize for shutting you out." His eyes flicked up, and Hannah's gaze followed, even though she knew exactly what she'd find.

Mistletoe.

The corner of Ben's mouth tipped into a half-smile. "That's the kind of sorry I like." He slid his hands around her waist, making her heart thump against her ribs.

Stiffening, she muttered, "After this, we are going to actually talk."

"Oh, I intend to."

Hannah steeled herself for an embarrassing display, especially as relatives had begun to gather in the periphery. She was kissing Santa Claus after all. Ben moved his hands from her waist to her neck, cradling her face. He passed his thumbs over her cheekbones and leaned in.

His lips hovered a fraction above hers. "You still want to talk?"

She wanted this, the balance of passion and persuasion, weakness and strength that he made her feel. Hannah closed the distance between their lips herself.

Kissing him was like finding home—like placing magnolia and mistletoe on The Hideaway's tables and seeing how perfect the arrangement set the ambiance. Like soft candlelight and lapping waves and all the joy of Christmas morning.

There was still much to say. Much to know and discover and confront. But in that moment, as he pulled his beard away so he could mold her lips unencumbered, Hannah knew they had found their own moment of belonging.

Their own happily ever after.

A Note from the Author

I hope you enjoyed reading this taste of an Edisto Christmas as much as I enjoyed writing it! Celebrations down South revolve around three things: food, faith, and family. It's a delight to show you a little of our culture through Hannah and Ben's story.

I also hope, if you haven't read Cora Anne's story, you'll consider purchasing <u>Still Waters</u> for yourself or a friend. My debut novel is infused with my own family's history and ties to Edisto Island, South Carolina, and yes, it's a real place. If you're interested in learning more about Edisto, its beach, history, and adventures, I suggest visiting <u>ExploreEdisto.com</u>.

Once more, thank you for being one of my readers! I am deeply humbled that would you take the time when there are so many wonderful books out there. If you're interested in my TBR shelf, you can follow me on Instagram <u>@lindseypbrackett</u> or like my Facebook page, <u>Lindsey P. Brackett</u>. I love hearing from you and gleaning even more book suggestions from your comments.

Have the merriest Christmas, friends, whether your wreath is magnolia or evergreen, whether you have snow or sunshine, whether you're celebrating with friends or family, I wish you all the joy of this season that is found in Christ alone.

Oh, and if you get caught under the mistletoe, may your happily ever after be exactly what you're hoping.

Merry Christmas!
Lindsey